When Harry met Saffy

the start of something Big

by Lynn Morsy & Hannah Smart

authorHOUSE

AuthorHouse™ UK
1663 Liberty Drive
Bloomington, IN 47403 USA
www.authorhouse.co.uk
Phone: UK TFN: 0800 0148641 (Toll Free inside the UK)
*   UK Local: (02) 0369 56322 (+44 20 3695 6322 from outside the UK)*

Published by AuthorHouse 05/04/2022

ISBN: 978-1-6655-9692-3 (sc)
ISBN: 978-1-6655-9693-0 (hc)
ISBN: 978-1-6655-9691-6 (e)

For the hoomans who made our mummies who they are today,
to every black cat in the world, we want to say ...

This is for you.

Introduction

My name is Harry, and my best friend is Saffy. We have made our story about our paw adventures together when we became special cat agents and went on a very big journey to meet Professor Maurice Mole, Bert the beefburger, and the dreaded rattus rattus. When our mummies found out about our paw adventure, they wanted to write about it in this bookeee for all hoomans to read! Our mummies said it is a story of two best friends' adventure and it will make hoomans giggle and take away the stress of everyday hooman life. We hope you purrrrr it as much as we do!

1

Calamity Strikes!

Harry squinted as he sat on the dining room windowsill and looked into the bright, sunny day. His green eyes glistened, and his glossy black coat warmed in the sun. It was an exciting garden, he thought, with its little privet hedges that made circles and squares for him to run around. He had lived here in Berkyshire, in the Croweland, for five years. He knew no other place. It was a peaceful, sleepy place, Croweland. Nothing much happened there—apart from when one of his neighbours got a new kitty, and sometimes there was a kitty scrap—but it usually settled down again. He was very happy with his family. He arrived as small bundle of black fluff and had grown into a sleek and elegant black steed. Some thought black cats were unlucky. Harry's mummy didn't. She thought he was just wonderful. He knew this because she bought him lots of lovely Happeelix treats and gave him lots of cuddles, which he *adored*!

His mummy also loved dogs. Several doggos also lived in his house. They were hairy, white doggos and looked a bit like his mummy, who had long, white hair. They were a bit daft, like his mummy, who often forgot things. Once she forgot his Happeelix! Harry called them the dirty dogs as they always seemed to have mud and leaves attached to their hair.

THE DIRTY DOGS

Earlier, Harry went looking for his mummy and couldn't find her anywhere! Had she forgotten to tell him that she was going shopping? He didn't know quite what to do. He thought hard, and it made his whiskers twitch. Who could he ask for help? *I know*, he thought. *I will Pawtime Saffy!*

Saffy was smart! She was a sassy black cat who lived with his mummy's friend Hanny on a farm in the countryside. His mummy met Hanny over the Spiders Web during the big lockdown. The mums had become firm friends and introduced Harry and Saffy to each other through Pawtime. Harry longed to meet Saffy whisker to whisker, but it had not been possible so far.

He would Pawtime Saffy. She would know what to do. Saffy had taught him all about Pawtime! He *loved* seeing her on Pawtime! He jumped from the windowsill to the table where the box lived, the box that showed pictures and where the Spiders Web lived. It also made Pawtime work.

But Pawtime was not working!

Why? he wondered, scowling at the box in which the Spiders Web lived. "Come on, spiders. Come on, paws."

Was there a problem with the Spiders Web? Was it the lickelectricity?

"Check the plug," Saffy had often said. So he checked. After all, Saffy is a very smart cat.

Dalmatians! The lickelectricity switch was off! He pushed it hard with his button nose. *Click.* It was on!

"Saffy, are you there?"

"What is it, Harry?"

"She has *gone*, Saffy!"

"Who, Harry?"

"Mummy."

"Where?"

"Away, away."

"OK, Harry, first things first. You need to calm down. She will be back. Your mummy might have just gone to the spaaaaaaaa place. Have you checked to see if she's taken her trainers? Maybe she has gone to the holiday shoppee to get you some tinned sardines or custard. Have you been watching out the windows? Did you see her go? When my mummy goes missing, I go to my special watching place, sit on my plushy chair, and check outside to see if she is in her Pawschee car."

Harry thought about what Saffy had said. He hadn't seen his mummy go out. Had he been dozing?

Saffy continued, "Have you checked all the normal signs? Is her big case still there? Has she taken her furbrush?"

"Yes, yes, Saffy. I will go and check all these things you have suggested, but I didn't see her leave the house, you know." Harry went around the room, looking for clues.

"Saffy! I found an envelope with my name on it! It's here on the table, near the box."

"Open it, Harry. It might tell you what has happened to your mummy."

Harry clawed at the envelope and a piece of paper fell out. It said:

Dear Harry,

I'm very sorry. I have to say
that I have had to go away.
You might shout and flick your tail.
When you find out, you'll scratch your nails.
Mummy had to go up north.
She's trying very hard, of course.
The dirty dogs are in a show,
and alas, dear Harry, I've had to go!

The dirty dogs, they need their bows
and ribbons and glitter for their shows.
Their bouncy coats, their fluffy faces,
Mummy really wants to win first place.
Oh, Harry, you know I love you so.
I'm sorry; you must stay with Daddy Mo.
It won't be long till I come to fix
your sad eyes, Harry, with Happeelix.

Love,
Mummy x

What! thought Harry. *She has gone with the dirty dogs to a dirty dog show and left me here?* Not all the dirty dogs had gone. He was sure of it! Two of them were still in the house. He could see them through the glass in the door to the kitchen.

how
could
she
leave?

Harry turned his attention back to the box and stared hard at Saffy. His green eyes were like saucers! He was scared, very scared. He didn't know what was happening. He hadn't experienced this feeling before.

"What should I do, Saffy? My tail is all in a quiver; even my whiskers are quivering. Everything is quivering! She has gone away with the dirties. I don't know when she will be back!" cried Harry.

"Harry, I will sort this out! You can't be quivering. It is not good for you. It will give you furballs again. I will talk to Mummy and see if she will send the Pawschee car! You will stay with us, Harry."

Harry was thrilled! After all this time talking to Saffy, he was going to stay with her and her mummy on the farm. Everything would be OK! He was sure of it. "Thank you, Saffy. You are the best. I would *love* to come and stay with you and your mummy," he said in his best and happiest voice.

"Harry, this will be such fun," Saffy said. Harry knew when she was getting serious because the tiny little tips of her dainty ears rose. He knew it was time for Saffy's words of wisdom.

"Harry, let me tell you a little story that might help you with your quivering tail. I have noticed that when you get very worried then very excited and then very sad, your tail goes up and down—happy, sad, happy, sad. Sometimes in life, Harry, you need to lie sideways and let your whiskers touch the ground. Then instead of your tail going up, down, up, down, it just sways from side to side. It'll make you feel much happier, like the wind is blowing gently through your fur. I have listened to Mummy talk about this, Harry, on the Aunty Julie coaching calls. The hoomans do it when they talk about their 'busyness.' We must learn from the clever mums."

So that was what Harry did, and he felt better straightaway!

Suddenly the Pawtime cut out! The box went black and buzzed like a bumblebee.

"Saffy, where have you gone?" cried Harry. He banged his paws on the box—nothing! The box stayed black and *buzzzzzzzzzzzzzzed*!

2

The Lion Roars

Harry had a strange feeling in his bones. His black fur frizzled from his head to his tail. Something suddenly didn't feel right. So he looked around quickly from where he was sitting. And to his surprise, he was not alone anymore. Lion was staring straight at him through the open kitchen door!

Lion stared, his golden eyes glistening in the sun. It was a hard, cold stare that spooked Harry. Lion's golden-brown fur shone in the morning light. He looked big with his bushy tail. He lived in the house next to Harry's house, and Harry found him to be a very grumpy cat. Lion was often heard growling and yowling in the night to anyone who would listen to him. And Harry was *sure* that no one had the choice but to listen to him! During the day, Lion prowled around the gardens in Harry's street, looking in hoomans' rubbish bins. Harry had seen him doing so when he took his own walk out. Harry always kept away from him. He didn't want to get mixed up with that sort of cat at all.

But at this moment, Harry wasn't sure what to do. His tail twitched nervously.

"Hello, Lion," he mumbled, looking away as he spoke. He didn't want to make Lion cross by looking in his eyes.

"Harry, I am *hungry*. There is nothing in the bins today! I want *your* fud! Where is it?" Lion said. Then he let out a big, loud hiss.

"It's in the kitchen, but you can't come in."

"Really?" Lion purred. "You just watch me!"

And then Lion jumped into the kitchen and went towards the fud bowl containing some of Harry's breakfast leftovers. There really wasn't much there at all.

Crikey, thought Harry. *If the dirty dogs see him in the house, they will be so angry they will chase him for sure!* And then as if by magic, the dirties appeared.

The next few seconds were a blur of white fur as the dirty dogs flew out of the hall, into the kitchen, around the gravel path, and back into the kitchen. Lion roared. His fur fluffed out so he looked *three* times his normal size! The dirty dogs (who were white Coton de Tulears, full of fluff but always with a grey tinge to their fur, and usually with leaves and bits of grass attached to them), ran straight at Lion. But the Lion was quick. He turned quickly, dashed out of the kitchen, and raced off down the garden!

Harry was so relieved. The dirty dogs turned to Harry and grinned! "That OK for you, Harry mate?" "Did that do the trick??"

"Oh *yes*, thank you, dirties." They still made him nervous, but they did have their uses!

The dirties bounced off back into the kitchen, grinning at each other! "Good chase, mate," one of the dirties said.

"Yeh, can't beat a good chase, mate," replied the second one. "Let's go back to chewing our bones, yeh!"

The dirty dogs had saved the day!
They had chased Lion away,
Away from Harry's favourite food,
Cheering Harry into a better mood.
They certainly knew how to scare that cat!
The dirty dogs are where it's at!

3

The Great Escape

Harry returned to the box on the table in the dining room. Suddenly, the box started pinging again. It had come back to life. It was Saffy on Pawtime.

"Harry, the Pawschee is coming for you. We will be together!"

Harry gulped. He had heard about the Pawschee from Saffy before, and he was a little worried. He knew it was *very* fast and *very* loud. *Will I be OK?* he wondered. His tail quivered.

"Oh, Saffy, will it be OK?"

"There is no other way to get here Harry," said Saffy. "You will be OK if you curl up tight and wrap your tail around your ears. Mummy will make sure you are OK. Just be brave!"

Harry waited. How long would Saffy's mummy be?

Harry looked out his window. The sky was getting cloudy now, blocking out some of the sun. If he stretched his neck, he could just see the drive to the house. He was sure the pawshee was getting close, but would Saffy's mummy remember where he lived?

His next problem was to distract Daddy Mo, so he wouldn't see him escaping and try to stop him. Daddy Mo was very kind, but it wasn't the same as being with his mummy. Daddy Mo was always on the box or looking after the dirty dogs. Harry felt Daddy Mo was just too busy to fuss over him.

The sunshine broke through the clouds, and Harry planned to do one last check of the garden to make sure his mummy's weeds were OK and to see the balloon clownfish in the pond.

Daddy Mo was busy playing a hooman mousey game on the sofa, so he didn't hear Harry sneak onto the kitchen worktop to his Happeelix jar. Harry knew that he couldn't meet Saffy for the first time without taking her the grass and liver custard. That was her favourite. He pawed into the jar. *My claws need trimming,* Harry thought. He couldn't paw them with his pads, and he didn't want Daddy Mo to hear him. So one by one, he picked a selection of Happeelix out with his teeth and threw them onto the kitchen floor. Would five be enough for Saffy? Seven would be better. Two more. Done!

Harry jumped off the worktop.

"Harrryyyy, where are you?" Oh, whiskers. It was Daddy Mo! Harry scuttled the Happeelix under the cupboard and ran to see him. He knew if he got to him before he got off the sofa, Daddy Mo would probably go straight back to his mousey game on his mini box.

"Meowwww, meoowww. Purrrrrrrrerr. Purrrr. Purr. Yes, Daddy Mo, *purrrr,* I love you too. *Purr. Meow."*

Right. Daddy Mo's attention left him, and Harry ran back to the kitchen and to the worktop. He had to open the kitchen door. He pushed his tail, fur side up, against the kitchen tiles. They were chilly. One, two, three, jump.

Harry had only tried this manoeuvre once before. Luckily, he caught the handle with his paw, and as he started to slip down to the shiny blue and white floor, the door gently popped open. Harry could smell the wet grass in the garden. Yes! He was free. He ran over the grass to the drive. He would wait for the pawshee and Hanny, Saffy's mummy.

4

The Pawschee

ROARRRR.....

As Harry sat by the blue garage door, with its peeling paint, he wondered why his mummy hadn't painted it again. *Maybe she forgot,* he mused. Then suddenly, he was jolted out of his thoughts as he heard a loud *roar*. He backed up towards the garage door. He felt like a sardine in a little tin can, and he immediately felt guilty at how sardines must feel in the holiday shoppee.

Its eyes were black, as black as night.
When it growled, it gave a fright!
Its mouth was wide; its teeth were few,

Its coat was black, like Harry's hue!
This beast—A lion? A tiger or a bear?
Harry was not sure, he must declare!
It rumbled as it came up near,
Poor Harry's whiskers shook with fear.
The black eyes changed from black to "glow".
It rumbled gently, stopping slow.
One big *click*, its wheel's turn,
And Harry's tummy started to churn.
The beast gave an almighty roar.
Poor Harry's tummy on the floor.
Then it purrrredddd its final growl.
He was starting to feel calmer now.
Click; the beast opened its paw.
To Harry's delight, Saff's mum he saw.
She left the beast; her eyelids flickered,
And Harry's heart was all a'whiskered!

Saffy's mummy walked up his garden path. She looked lovely and just as Saffy described, with long, brown fur and pink claws. He gazed at her, his green eyes getting bigger and bigger with delight!

"Hello, Harry," she said with a purr. "Are you ready? Do you want to bring your Happeelix with you?"

Harry didn't know what to say. He gazed at her and then rolled on his back, twitching his paws with delight. Then he did his best circling around her legs and *purrrred* as much as the Pawschee had.

"OK, Harry. Let's go." Saffy's mummy walked towards the Pawschee and opened the door.

Harry poked his nose in. It smelled very different, very exotic. He decided it was now or never, so he jumped in.

He sat in the front seat. It felt very big! So he did as Saffy had said and curled up tight, his tail over his ears.

The Pawschee growled as it started. Harry peeped over his tail and saw the binocular button that Saffy told him about a few Pawtimes before. This button would make the Pawschee roar. Would Saffy's mum press it?

16

The Pawschee glided down the road on the way to Saffy's house. Harry was on the move for the first time ever!

Harry realised he couldn't see anything with his tail over his ears and eyes. He was curious. This wasn't bad! He had to know what was happening, so he stretched up and looked out the window. *Wow, this is amazing!* He was passing trees and fields so quickly. *This is exciting,* he thought. He was the king of the road!

"Do you like this, Harry? Is it fun?" asked Saffy's mummy.

Harry purred with delight. *Purr.*

The next thing he knew, the tin-can roof of the Pawschee was opening. *Oh, this is exciting,* he thought. He could feel the sun on his fur and smell the different smells as they sped along.

Harry hummed to himself and purred a little song:

> Purrrrreee, hee, hee, here I am on the open road.
> Nothing to be scared of! Nothing to be scared of!
> Away we go, ho, ho, ho,
> Off to see my Saffyyyyyy at the fancy farm.
> Only fun and frolics, nothing to fear or harm!

"We are nearly there, Harry. Shall I press the binoculars button?"

Harry thought hard! Well, he was sure it would be OK. Everything else had been OK. He purred loudly. Next came the roar of the binoculars, and it was magnificent! He was so pleased he had been brave because this was so much fun!

The Pawschee slowed down again as it turned into the driveway of the farm. "We are here, Harry," Saffy's mummy announced. And sure enough, there was Saffy, waiting for him in the courtyard. She looked lovely, just as he knew she would.

They were together at last!

5

The Arrival

Harry could not get out of the car. She was there, sitting on the doormat with a picture of a heart on it. It was her. His Saffy.

Saffy's mummy looked at her and did a squinty eye. Saffy did one back. She licked her paw and swept it so beautifully behind her ear twice. Harry had seen those ears on Pawtime, but he couldn't believe how elegant and delicate Saffy's ear tips were.

Harry had to collect himself. He gulped hard and licked his paw, giving it a gentle bite to remind himself that it was reality! He also suddenly remembered that he had missed his mummy. But that seemed a lifetime ago.

"Come on, Harry. Don't be shy," said Saffy's mum. "Saffy doesn't bite. And nor do I! Do you want me to lift you out of the car, or are you going to do it yourself?"

Crikey, she was right. Harry needed to get his fur straight. He had sat there gaping at poor Saffy with his tongue out. She was a cougar, and he needed to show her that he was there for her and that he would look after her.

He stretched up on his back legs. Harry used his long and slender tail to flick the cat belt undone. Saffy's mummy still had the tin lid off the pawshee, so he used his powerful back legs to jump on the windscreen ledge to get a good look at his Saffy. And she could see how excited he was to see her!

Saffy's mummy brought Harry's Happeelix and his mousey toy, and Harry started to stretch a long stretch, a downward facing cat, across the windscreen. His pads slipped a bit on the Pawschee glass, but he managed to arch and stretch his back.

As Harry got to his tail stretch,

one

vertebrae

at

a

time,

making sure she was watching him, his pads slipped beyond all control, and he clumsily roly-polyed down the glass windscreen thing and on to the bonnet hat.

Oh, whiskers.

Saffy sat giggling on the doormat. Harry could see her little blushing whiskers as she hid behind her paw.

6

Everything's Different

Harry looked around him as he slowly walked over to Saffy. Her house was very different from his own. His house had two levels, whereas Saffy's had one level and was right next to the farm's fields. The road to her house was down a long and winding road, with trees and fields on either side, to get to her house. His house was close to other houses and the road.

The heavy wooden door was open. Harry could see right inside the house with its wooden floors. He was nervous because he never went into other people's houses. Mummy had warned him not to do that as you might get shut in by mistake or catnapped.

"Come on, Harry. Come in, and I will show you everything," cried a very excited Saffy, who was spinning on the spot, her tail waving madly.

"Here is the comfy place where we can play games and use the box and watch the picture box and play horsey and eat our snax and play with the cushions and …" Saffy was so excited she couldn't stop talking. She jumped from the luxurious pink sofa to a spotty cow skin lounge chair.

PURRRRRRR !!!

"This is my tower, Harry, where I sometimes sleep and sometimes play games with Mummy," Saffy proudly proclaimed. Harry looked to see a tall cat tower with a scratching post and secret bed in soft grey wool. It looked like the ideal place to lounge around in all day. It was situated next to the window, so he would have a perfect view of the world outside.

"Here is the kitchen. Harry, Harry, keep up!" shouted Saffy as she dashed off around the big table into the kitchen. "This is where the Happeelix lives, and where we get all our fud!"

Harry suddenly remembered he had brought some Happeelix for her. Where was it? Was it still in the Pawschee? Saffy jumped on to the worktop with a flick of her tail. "Ooooo, Harry, what's this? Is this Happeelix for me?" Saffy's mummy had brought it in from the car and put it on the kitchen worktop. *Phew*, thought Harry. *It's OK. It's here!*

"Yes, it's for you Saffy. I brought it with me as a present. it's your favourite flavour—liver and catgrass."

"Harry, you *are* a gentleman, I shall put it in my special jar, where all my Happeelix stays. And, of course you can have some of it too." Saffy carried the Happeelix one by one to a large round bowl. It was a beautiful bowl with pale pink flowers on a blue background and with green leaves. Harry knew it was in the style of William Morris, so it was a very special bowl indeed.

Harry noticed that pictures of him and Saffy that Saffy's mummy had drawn were on top of the wood burny box. *Ah, that's lovely,* he thought. *She must really like me to have my picture next to hers.*

Saffy ran down the corridor as Harry was staring out the large patio windows. He thought they must open out to the garden. He could see the garden with flowers and steps up to the lawn. It looked like a great place to explore. He also noticed something strange. It looked like a small house with wire all the way round it. Behind it were trees and bushes. Harry wasn't sure what this could be. *Why would you have a small house like that in your garden place?* he wondered. He would have to ask Saffy. She would know.

He followed Saffy down the long corridor to the door which opened into the bedroom. Harry's eyes widened. *This is a huge bed,* he thought, *much, much bigger than I have at home.* He looked under the bed to see if Saffy was there. He stared really hard. *What is this?* he wondered. He stretched a paw under the bed and touched it. It was soft and fuzzy. And it moved when he touched it again. But it wasn't alive!

"Saffy, Saffy. Where are you?" he cried. "I found something strange under the bed!" Saffy ran to see what Harry was talking about. She peered under the bed. "Saffy, what is it? I don't think it's alive. Is it?"

Saffy looked again and started giggling. "It's a dust monster, Harry. They live under the bed and behind the sofa and chairs!" Mummy isn't very good at catching them, Harry, so they come and live here. It won't harm you. Sometimes they make you sneeze!"

Harry breathed a sigh of relief! *Nothing to worry about then,* he thought and withdrew from under the bed.

"Harry, come and see our bedroom's blanket tower. It's great, and from there we can watch everything!" Saffy jumped on the chest of drawers and then up to the top of the wardrobe. There were layers and layers of blankets, all in different colours and neatly folded, with Saffy on top! "No one can get up here, Harry," Saffy said with a snort.

Harry looked up and hoped he wouldn't knock them all over when he jumped up! The he decided to leave the blanket tower for another day. He had already embarrassed himself getting off the Pawschee.

"Oh, well, let's go and see all the other places in the house then, Harry." Saffy leapt down. She ran out of the bedroom and back down the corridor. She headed off to the human washing place. Harry followed her, eager to see what strange things might live in that room.

"Saffy, what is that in the garden?" asked Harry.

"Not now, Harry. You need to see the human washing place first," Saffy bossed him. "Harry, feel the floor. What does it feel like?"

That's a strange question, thought Harry as he tentatively walked across the tile. They were *warm*! He had never experienced that feeling, and it was lovely.

"Yes, Harry, we have a hot floor! And a snuggle mat," said Saffy proudly. "Do you like it?"

"Wonderful, Saffy! But what is in the garden, in that small house?"

"Not now, Harry. I will show you later. It's getting dark now, and it's best to see it in the daylight, when the rattigans have gone to bed."

7

The Welcome Party

Harry was quite worn out after his ride in the Pawschee and exploring the house. He curled up on the velvet armchair and took a power nap.

Saffy wasn't tired *at all*. She had big plans!

Her whiskers and tail twitched with excitement. Her beautiful yellow eyes narrowed in thought. *Yes, I know what to do to show Harry a good time.* She had watched her mummy party and have fun. She would do the same for Harry. This was such an important night for her. It was her first night with Harry. They had Pawtimed for ages, and now he was here with her!

She padded into the kitchen and looked around. Where were the snax? Ah, she remembered they were in the beautiful Happeelix pot. *That's OK,* she thought. *We will have them.*

Then she sat down and thought hard. *Where was the bubbly wine she had seen Mummy drink?* She would find some and give it to Harry in the beautiful glasses Mummy used.

Saffy jumped on the kitchen worktop and looked around. Where were the bubbles?

Then she saw it! The bubbly bottle was on the windowsill. She wondered, *How can I open it?* She had seen Mummy twist its top, and then she had heard it go *pop*! She wouldn't be able to do that; she didn't have thumbs.

She had an idea. She would push the bottle on its side, and then pick a hole in the cork!

She had time to make everything ready for the part while Harry rested. She got the Happeelix and some ham bites ready. Then she gently nudged the bottle, so it swayed and landed on its side. *Phew,* Saffy thought. *Now it's time to pick, pick, pick!*

But she couldn't find the special drinking glasses! So Saffy pushed her drinking bowl under the bottle. She started to pick at the cork with her long claws. Slowly, slowly, she made a little hole in the cork, and the bubbly wine dribbled into her bowl. Yes, success! She felt proud of her achievement. *Wait until Harry sees what I've done!*

She smiled. She had seen her mummy when she had drunk bubbles, and she had a great time! Mummy danced and giggled. Saffy wanted to do that with Harry. She padded back into the lounge to see what was happening with Harry.

"Harry, are you awake?" She purred. He looked so cute curled up on the pink settee.

He stretched his long black body and yawned. "Yes, Saffy, I am!"

"Harry, we are going to *partyeeee!*"

Harry was still trying to wake up when Saffy slipped into the human washing place. *Now, where does Mummy keep the pink claws stuff?*

She looked around the human washing place. The bottle of pink claws stuff was on the windowsill. She jumped up and knocked it down into the sink.

Smash! The bottle broke, and the pink claws stuff went into the sink. It was everywhere! *Never mind. Mummy will clean it up!* Saffy extended her claws and dipped them into the gooey pink paint! *Woweeee! Harry won't be able to resist me now!* She decided to just colour her front claws; that would be classy!

Saffy then looked around for some perfume. Her mummy always smelt lovely! She would use some. But when she couldn't find any, she decided she would smell of Happeelix instead. Harry would *adore* that.

Harry was still stretching as she went into the bedroom and found just what she was looking for! The pink scarf! She jumped on it and rolled around so it twisted around her body and tail. "Well, look at that," she said to herself as she looked in the mirror. "I look like a proper *lady.*"

Meanwhile, Harry had stretched enough and was now fully awake. He wasn't sure what a party was, but he thought he better look smart.

He started licking himself from top to toe. His coat gleamed in the early evening sun. He knew he looked good. "Well, Saffy", he said to himself, "I am ready for you, girl!"

Just at that moment, Saffy came out of the bedroom. She stood at the door, her tail twitching in the air, looking very pleased with herself all in pink!

She was beautiful ♡

Harry started to laugh. "Saffy, what have you done to yourself?"

"What?" screeched Saffy. "What do you mean, Harry?"

"Saffy, you look lovely without the pink scarf. You don't need that on."

Saffy sulked. She had made such an effort, and Harry was laughing at her!

"Come on, Saffy. Don't be cross." Harry purred. "Let me see your lovely furrrrrrr."

Saffy shook herself until the scarf came loose. She ran over to Harry. "Harry, look. I have got you some bubbles and snax for our party!"

Saffy took Harry over to her bowl with the bubbles in it. Harry sniffed it. He wasn't sure.

Saffy had already decided to have a good slurp of the bubbles, and her little pink tongue lapped the bubbles. "Oooo, Harry. These are fun! Look, the bubbles pop in your nose!"

Harry thought hard and then decided to try the bubbles. *Ahh*, he thought as the bubbles popped up his nose. But he kept drinking!

"Do you want some Happeelix, Harry?" asked a giggly Saffy.

"Oh, yes please, Saffy." They both went to the Happeelix bowl.

But just as they got there, their paws went wobbly. And Saffy rolled over on her back! "He, he, he! Harry, I can't feel my paws!"

"Neither can I, Saffy." They both started purring loudly.

"I know what will help, Harry. Let's play horsey," Saffy suggested with a giggle. "We run as fast as we can up and down the room. No one can stop us!"

So off they went, up and down the room. Or they thought they did! "Saffy, I don't think I am running. Are you?" murmured Harry.

"He, he, he, he. No, Harry. We haven't moved at all."

So there they lay, their paws like lead, wriggling on the floor.

Suddenly, the door crashed open. "What?" asked Harry and Saffy simultaneously.

The KFC, as Saffy called them, were in the kitchen.

"What's happening, Saffy?" asked Lady Grey. "We heard there is a partyeeee."

"Yes", answered Saffy. "But just for me and Harry." All romantic thoughts left her mind now that the KFCs were there.

The KFCs looked like dinosaurs as they strutted around the kitchen. They had beady eyes and long necks. And they had claws for feet. They looked very strong. *Do they live in the small house in the garden?* Harry wondered.

"So, Saffy, what is happening with this party?" a KFC asked and clucked loudly.

"The bubbles are in the dish," Harry muttered, turning his head towards the dish.

"Lovely, lovely, lovely", clucked the dinosaurs as they fluttered over to the dish.

"But", started Saffy. It was too late. Their beaks were *everywhere*—in the bubbles, in the Happeelix! The bubbles quickly vanished, as did the Happeelix!

Crikey, thought Harry. Then he noticed that Saffy had swayed off behind the pink sofa! He quickly—well, as quickly as his wibbly-wobbly paws allowed—went to her. "What's going to happen now, Saffy?" He meowed softly.

"Harry, I just don't know," replied Saffy, nearly crying. "I am quite, quite scared."

The next thing they knew, the dinosaurs were dancing around the kitchen, squawking and screeching as the bubbles took effect.

Harry and Saffy peeped out from the sofa cushions, horrified by what they saw!

The dinosaurs had started to pop out eggs all over the kitchen floor. Eggs rolled everywhere! "Saffy, what should we do?"

"Nothing, Harry," Saffy answered. "They will stop soon. Then we will collect the eggs and put them in a safe place."

But before they could do that, the dinosaurs started tripping over all the eggs. The shells cracked, and bright yellow yolks and slimy egg whites were everywhere.

"Girls, girls", screeched Lady Grey. "This is *disgusting!* It's such a mess, we can't stay here."

And with that the dinosaurs ran back out into the garden and back to their house.

Saffy and Harry came out from the sofa and *stared* at the mess!

Poor Saffy. Tears started to roll down her beautiful black cheeks. "Don't cry, Saffy. It will be all right," said Harry. "Mummy will fix it. Mummies always do! Let's go and curl up on your bedroom blanket tower. We will be safe there!"

Saffy sighed. "OK, Harry, if you think that's best."

So off they went. As they curled up safely, Harry thought, *Those bubbles, they made all this happen!* He would talk to Saffy about it in the morning, but until then, they would curl up tight on their first night together.

8

Dodgy Dinosaurs

Harry and Saffy were curled up together when they heard strange noises coming from the dinner place. "Harry, can you hear that noise? It sounds like a squeaky hoover," exclaimed Saffy.

"Saffy, do you think we should go and investigate? I'm really comfy, snuggling here with you. But I think we should just check that your mummy is OK."

"Good point, Harry. Let's go and see what is happening." And with that, Saffy curled her paws and stretched her back, gracefully performing a downward dog as she flicked Harry in the face with her tail. She really was a beautiful cat, and Harry was so pleased that she was his best friend, and he was safe here on the farm with her until his mummy came home.

They jumped down from the wardrobe to the orchid windowsill and over the hooman whirly wind-maker. They shimmied under the bed to the little dinner place ladder. Harry got some fluff stuck on his whiskers, and Saffy gently pawed it off for him. Saffy told him that her mum wasn't very good at hoovering. Harry watched the sunshine on her pretty whiskers, and he had to pinch his tail. *I wonder what would it be like if Saffy and I lived together all the time?*

"Harry, will you keep up please? That noisy thing is getting louder. It sounds like it is coming from the human washing place, and I can hear my mummy talking. Mummy, I'm coming to seeee you!"

Harry and Saffy skidded across the floor as they ran, their claws slippery on the wood floor. Harry wasn't used to it, and he overshot the hooman catflap by a few whiskers.

"Saffy, what is your mum doing over the bath? She looks a bit funny," asked Harry.

They sneaked into the human washing place. Saffy's mummy was leaning into the bath, kneeling on the snuggling mat. She must have had some cleaning stuff in the water place!

"*Squawkkkkkk!*"

"Saffy, what on earth was that?" exclaimed Harry.

Harry ran at his top speed, his tail going so fast that it was in front of his whiskers. He did not like this floor. He slid all the way across it, like the film he used to watch when he was a kitten of his cousin Tom and his friend Jerry. They had flooded the house, the floor froze, and they did the ice skating!

"Harry, where have you gone? You are such a scaredy cat. Come back. Don't worry. Come and see this because you will never believe your eyes," Saffy meowed. Then she squealed, "The dinosaur is in the bath!"

Harry could barely believe his ears. A dinosaur? On the farm? In the house? In the human washing place? In the bath? How would it fit? Then he remembered last night, and Saffy had called the chickens KFCs and dinosaurs!

He twitched his whiskers and shook his head. He needed to see this. He could feel his tail quivering. He knew he had to be strong for Saffy if she needed him! They crept back into the human washing place. Harry could feel the lovely warm floor on his pads. *When I get home, I will tell my mummy to put the radiators into the floor like Saffy has.*

"Mummy, what are you doing?" Saffy rubbed her head on her mummy's leg to check if she was OK. Then she stood on her hind legs, placing her front paws on the ledge of the bath. She looked back at Harry and squinted her eyes. She tried to stop her giggling and twitching her whiskers. "Harry, come and see this," she said in amazement.

Harry tentatively moved along the side of the wall, under the washing. He hid for a moment behind the bra thingies and the sockies. Then he stood and rested his paws next to Saffy's paws. There was a live KFC in the bath!

"Saffy, why does your mummy have a chicken in the bath?" he asked.

"Harry, that's Lady Grey. Mummy said she has an egg stuck inside her tummy, and she has to have a spa in Epsom salts to relax her tummy so that the big egg can come out. Then Mummy can make us some custard with it."

"Wasn't it Lady Grey who spoilt our party, Saffy?"

"Oh, yes, Harry, you are right!" exclaimed Saffy. "Maybe it was the bubbles that she drank that has made the egg stick inside her. We must be kind to her, Harry, as she is so poorly."

Umm, thought Harry, *that is big of Saffy, given how the dinosaurs made such a mess in the kitchen last night and then left the party.* He thought they were vandals and quite savage.

They watched Saffy's mum massage the KFC. Then she picked her up, wrapped her in a towel, and dried her off. Saffy's mum gave the KFC a cuddle and stroked her fur. Harry and Saffy watched whilst they enjoyed the warm floor. They stretched out to look like bananas and then decided to leave Saffy's mum to finish the KFC.

Harry could not wait to see his mummy and tell her all about this funny day he was having! *She will never, ever, ever believe it,* he thought. Little did he know that there was so much more to come. This was definitely the start of something big.

9

Mr Macavity

Harry still worried about his mummy. What was she doing and where? Was she safe? He don't like it when she left him even for a few hours. And it was worse when she was away for a long time, not that she really did that a lot. Actually, he couldn't remember the last time she was away from him. Not since the lockdown happened. After that, she had been home all the time! Harry didn't feel too well. It felt like a wasp had gone into his tummy fur and was buzzing around relentlessly.

Maybe it's time for me, he thought, trying to reassure himself. *It's good to have a little trip, isn't it?* He had met his Saffy, and his heart had done a flip. And he was experiencing all sorts of new smells.

Saffy said, "Enjoy the journey, Harry. Life is just way too short." Now he realised he knew it, and it was his time to court.

He had never met a cat like Saffy. No, not never in his life. She made his whiskers and tail shake. *Would she be my kitty wife?*

Harry was having all these thoughts when he suddenly heard, *Grrrrrrrrrrrr. Growlllll. Roarrrr.* What the fishes was that?

A snarly face, a grey-black stare,
Eyes like raisins with matted hair.
A wonky tail and a limping walk,
This ugly beast, how dare he talk?
He was huge, one strong back hind,

Dirty white, dirty grey, he was not kind.

He smelled of rats and stale pee,
Harry didn't not want his Saff to see
The way he leered and jeered and spat,
This Macavity was a dangerous cat.

Harry almost jumped out of his whiskers and hid behind Saffy. So brave, Harry. Good work. On the bed stood the beast.

"What are you doing with my Saffy?" he demanded.

"What?" Saffy asked.

Harry turned to Saffy, and she rolled her eyes. She looked back at Macavity and said, "Just leave us alone, old greybeard. This has nothing to do with you!"

Harry looked at her again. She already had a cat friend and hadn't told him? Why hadn't she? His tail started to quiver in panic, and he started to cough and sputter violently in shock. His Saffy. She had a boyfriend. Already!

His heart was racing like a butterfly bird. How could she do this to him? How could she lead him on after his mummy had left him?

He jumped off the poxy pillows, as he now saw them, and ran into the slippery floor place, looking for the door all in a panic. He walked past the love fud bowl he had sent to her, and he smashed it and the Happeelix into the floor. Why would mummy leave him, and why would Saffy do this to him as well?

"*Grrrrrrooowwwwlllll.*"

That big grey rhino cat was charging at Harry, his fur all fluffed up and puffy like the clownfish in his pond at home. Harry was shocked! He had to leave; there was nothing else to be done!

"Saffy, you and me, it's over! I'm going home to Daddy Mo!" Harry yelled. And with that, he ran at top speed out the door and past the dinosaurs, who started clucked loudly at him too.

"Where are you going, Harryyyy?" they called after him.

"Are you a scaredy cat, Harry?" mocked the big grey rhino cat. "Cat got your tongue, Harry? Have you got fleas, Harry?"

Harry sputtered and coughed and furballed in Lady Malcolm's face as he left the house. He ran as fast as he could away from her and the rest of the birds, their KFC feathers flapping all over the garden path! *She really is horrid,* he thought. He had been right after all about her and the KFCs. He would get away from all of them!

10

The Brief Encounter

Harry ran and ran without thinking where he was going. Through the trees and bushes at the bottom of the garden and through the long grasses, and was in a new garden with a beautiful lawn surrounded by roses.

Oh, bother. You don't know where you are. What were you thinking of? And you didn't even bring your cat nav!

When Harry had arrived there in the Pawschee, he was so excited that he hadn't checked the wind, the smells, his whiskers' sense, the cat nav. *Nothing.* And now he was lost! He remembered driving up a path road with some beefburgers on one side. Yes, that was where he had to go. But now, he was somewhere completely different.

He crept across the lawn that felt like velvet under his paws. He liked it here! It felt good, and his troubled mind started to ease.

The flower beds were full of beautiful snapdragons. He liked those flowers best as the bumblebees sneaked into them and then popped out having drunk the nectar. It looked so funny to him, like they were playing hide-and-seek. He was just about to pat the flower with his paw to see if anything would happen when he felt footsteps coming over the grass.

He jumped round, startled, and fluffed his tail up.

"Don't worry little lad," a soft voice said. "I won't hurt you. It's lovely to see you here. You are very welcome here!"

Harry looked up to see a tall, thin lady in a long white dress that had ruffles all the way down the skirt. She wore a huge hat to cover her long, curly, golden hair. *Who is this?* wondered Harry as the lady bent down to stroke him. She looked very kind, so Harry followed her up the lawn to the patio, where the lady had been sitting.

"Marge, what have you got there?" a man shouted from the open patio doors. "I have told you we are *not* having cats in the garden. They dig up the plants and mess everything up!"

"Oh, Henry", the lady replied, "he has found us. I will give him some food, so he will want to stay with us."

Harry gulped. He had heard about this sort of thing before; they called it catnapping. These types of people stole cats and kept them locked up. The catnappers made the cats live in their houses forever. The cats never played outside, never enjoyed the sun, never chased bumblebees, or anything like that. Harry started to back off from Marge.

"Come on, kitty. Come to Marge. Marge will look after you forrrrevvvverrrr," she whispered to him.

He ran to the flower bed and jumped in amongst the snapdragons! "Look, Marge," the man bellowed. "It's doing exactly what I said it would do. It's messing in the garden!"

Harry knew he had to get away as fast as he could. He didn't want to be a house cat. He had to find a way back to the farm and to Saffy. He no longer cared that she had a boyfriend. All he knew was he didn't want to be Marge's house cat.

By chance he found himself back amongst the trees and the long grasses at the bottom of Saffy's garden. He could smell the KFCs and where Saffy had walked before. He was in the right place. He lowered his back and ears and crept back into the farm's garden.

"Harry, you are back," screeched Lady Grey. "Did you meet the dreaded Marge? She looks like an angel, but she is the devil in disguise, you know! She wanted to eat us for lunch when she came to visit the farm last!"

Harry didn't reply. He stuck his tail in the air, wishing Marge had eaten Lady Grey and her birdbrain friends.

He decided that he had to face Saffy and tell her what he thought about it all. He would see if he could get a message to his mummy to find out if Daddy Mo could come and take him home. He had enough of all this adventure!

As he approached the kitchen door, he could see Saffy waiting for him. She had a worried look in her golden eyes. Her ears were flat against her head, and her tail was wrapped around her body.

"Where did you go Harry? I have been really worried! Did you go through the garden into Marge's den? I should have told you not to go that way *ever*!"

"Well, you didn't, did you, Saffy," snapped Harry. "You and your boyfriend let me go. You were too busy with *him* to care about *me*, Saffy."

"That's just not true Harry. And he is *not* my boyfriend. Mr Macavity makes trouble wherever he goes. I am sorry if you thought that, Harry. You are my best friend. I am sorry that you are upset"

Harry thought on this … but not for long. He would believe Saffy. He didn't want to stop having adventures with her, and he would get his own back on Mr Macavity. But maybe not just yet.

"Saffy, let's not talk about this anymore. Let's go and have some treats and play mousey on the box. That's always good fun!"

So off they went into the house. *Another life I have lost,* thought Harry as he curled up with Saffy. Never mind. He had quite a few left!

11

The Beefburgers

Harry woke up with a start! Where was he? The pillows smelt new and different. Then he remembered he was with his Saffy!

All those months he had dreamed about being with her! All those months Pawtiming, playing mousey, and sending her little presents. He was here *now*!

He looked at her curled up, asleep. She looked so sweet and glamorous as her pink claws showed beneath her shiny, jet-black fur. "Saffy," he whispered, "are you asleep?" *What a silly question?* Of course, she was! He rolled around on the cushions that felt so soft and lovely.

His movements woke Saffy up. "Morning, Harry," she purred. "Would you like to go out exploring today?"

"Oh, yes please. Saffy, where will we go?"

"I think we should go to the garden and then to see the beefburgers. We won't go through to Marge's den though!" Harry really didn't need reminding of his encounter with Marge. He shook the memories from his head and followed Saffy. They went through the glass doors, up the steps, and into the garden.

The garden was full of flowers and new smells for Harry. He spotted the dinosaurs in the corner of the garden. They were in their special house, the one Saffy's mummy made for them. Sensing Harry's nervousness, she explained, "It's OK, Harry. They can't get out yet. Mummy needs to open their door."

They walked around the garden, looking at all the flowers. Harry tried to remember where he was going, but his memory was no good at these things. So he just followed Saffy.

Down the lane they went, Saffy with her tail held high. "We shall see the beefburgers, Harry," she proclaimed. Sure enough, halfway down the lane they saw a herd of enormous black cows! "We call them the beefburgers, Harry. Let's go and say hello."

They padded off into the field. The ground felt damp and soggy to Harry as his paws sunk into the muddy grass. "Is this OK, Saffy?" he murmured. "It feels awfully strange to my paws."

"Oh, yes, Harry. Come on. We are nearly there!"

As they got near the beefburgers, Saffy suddenly squealed, "Harry, Harry. I think I'm stuck!" Her paws were deep in the muddy ground, and her legs and paws were disappearing fast!

The beefburgers moved slowly towards them, wondering what all the commotion was. "Saffy, youuuuuu OK?" mooed one of the beefburgers. "Where have your legs gone?"

Saffy cried, "No, Bert. I am *stuck*! What can I do?"

Harry stood there in dismay! *Crikey, what is going to happen now?* he wondered.

Bert moved closer to Saffy and dipped his head towards the mud. "Mmm, Saffy, I will dig you out with my horn! You need to keep very still. I won't hurt you!"

Saffy had no choice but to keep still. She was so stuck she wasn't going anywhere!

Bert got closer and dug his horn into the mud, just under where Saffy stood. He lifted his head, and suddenly Saffy was up in the air. Her little furry body lay across his horn!

"Wait, Saffy. Keep still, and I will put you somewhere safe." He walked towards the path. Saffy clung into Bert's horn with her muddy paws, trembling with fear.

Then Bert lowered his head, and Saffy jumped from his horn into the path. She was safe but very, very muddy.

"We only came to say hello, Bert. I wanted to introduce you to Harry. He is staying with us at the farm whilst his mummy is away at the Dirty Dog Show," she murmured. "I am so sorry to put you to all that trouble."

"Don't worry, Saffy," replied Bert. "Next time, Pawtime me, and we will walk to the path to see you. That way, you don't need to go in the mud."

"OK, Bert. That's good advice. We will Pawtime you. And thanks so much for saving me!"

As they waved their tails at Bert, Harry and Saffy walked back to the house. "We will have our breakfast now, Harry," commented Saffy. Harry thought she was very brave to think about food at a time like that! He didn't think he could. But they were safe, and that was all that mattered, he reflected, and then he wondered what was for breakfast.

Saffy's mummy greeted them at the door! "Good gosh, Saffy!" she cried. "What have you been doing?" Before Saffy could respond, her mummy had scooped her up in her arms and was walking quickly towards the human washing place.

The next thing Saffy knew, she was in the bath, up to her legs in water! She hated it as her mummy washed off the mud. The water was black. Saffy stood there in shock! *This is worse than being in the mud,* she thought.

"Come on, Saffy. Let's dry you now. Be a good girl, and you can have some Happeelix!"

Saffy's mummy got out the drying machine, and next thing Saffy knew, the blowing machine was on her, and her fur was becoming all fluffy! Harry laughed as Saffy's fur got bigger and bigger! "Don't laugh, Harry," Saffy shouted. "It's not funny!" But Harry couldn't help himself and laughed more!

Saffy decided enough was enough. She jumped away and raced down the corridor, doing her horsey moves.

"Happeelix time," she cried. And soon enough, the liver Happeelix was there! It was hers and Harry's favourite, and they danced around until Saffy's mummy had given them both *two* Happeelix each! *This is a good breakfast,* Harry thought. *But what on earth is going to happen to us next?*

12

A Rainy Afternoon

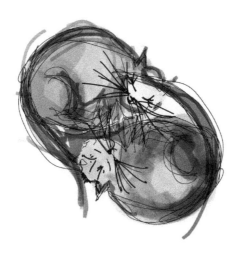

Saffy had been prowling around the living room. It was raining hard that afternoon, and she was bored. "Harry, Harry! What shall we do? It's raining!"

"We can go out, Saffy, and play like we're fishing in the puddles. It will be great fun," suggested Harry.

"What?" shrieked Saffy. "Are you mad, Harry? I will get my fur wet. I have just put a special gloss on it, and it will be ruined! And I don't want to go under the drying machine again!"

Heck, thought Harry, *I shouldn't have mentioned that one.* "What would you like to do, Saffy?" He asked.

"Well Harry, I would like to shop on the box," she purred

"What? Can we do that? I don't know how to do that," replied Harry

"I know," proclaimed Saffy. She ran off to the table where the box sat. She switched it on, and it seemed to go *buzzzzzzz.*

Harry jumped. His ears twitched nervously, and his eyes were like green saucers!

"It's working, Harry. Come and have a look." Saffy swished her tail excitedly.

Harry jumped up on the table and cautiously approached the box. He could see that it was working. He could see pictures of Happeelix and treats on the screen.

"I know how to buy these," Saffy proclaimed haughtily. "I do it all the time," she boasted.

Crikey, thought Harry, *Saffy knows so much. I need to learn so much!*

Saffy stared longingly at the screen. "I want them all," she purred. "Every one of them and more." Harry wasn't sure if she was talking to him; she seemed in her own world. Saffy's tailed twitched back and forth, back and forth.

Harry wasn't sure what was going to happen next. Then suddenly, Saffy started dancing and stamping on the box's keyboard. "I am getting them all, Harry. All of them!" She purred loudly.

Wow! thought Harry. *Is that how you do it?*

"When will they arrive, Saffy?" he asked.

"This afternoon, Harry. I paid extra so we would get them immediately!" She was very pleased with herself. She jumped down from the box and started to play horsey up and down the room on her own. "Come on, Harry. Join in. Let's do horsey." So Harry followed Saffy around the room, up and down the corridor, and back around the room.

"Phew, Saffy. Let's have a little rest," Harry said with a gasp as he curled up on a wonderful pink cushion.

"Oh, Harry, really?" Saffy scoffed. But it seemed a good idea, so she joined him and snuggled down.

The next thing Harry knew, someone was banging in the door. "Saffyyyyyyy, wake up, wake up. Someone is at the door."

Saffy was already up and at the door. She jumped at the handle, and it sprung open. Then box after box after box was brought into the house. The pile of boxes were growing into a very tall tower. "Crikey, Saffy, how much did you buy?" he asked.

"I bought the lot, Harry." Saffy giggled.

"What will your mummy say, Saffy?" Harry gulped.

"She will be fine, Harry. She is always buying stuff. I have *seen* her doing it, you know." Saffy giggled.

Two towers of boxes were now in the room, and a third was being built. After the fourth tower was completed, the men left. Harry and Saffy stared up at the towers. "Uh, Saffy, how do we open them?" asked Harry. He couldn't see how they could.

"We run and jump at them, Harry. Come on, let's do it," Saffy said confidently.

Harry watched as Saffy walked down the corridor, turned, and then ran full pelt at the boxes. The boxes crashed to the floor. And some of them burst op en!

Happeelix was *everywhere*! Harry was stunned but excited at the same time. "Here you go Harry," purred Saffy as she picked one the Happeelix open and pushed the rest of the Happeelix all over the kitchen floor. She and Harry sucked up the gorgeous juices. It covered their whiskers and their paws and their noses!

After fifteen minutes of eating the Happeelix, Saffy and Harry started to feel a bit sick. "Oooooo, Harry. I feel like I am going to explode!"

"Oh, don't say that, Saffy. I feel the same."

And just then, who should come through the door but Mr Macavity. "What's been going on here?" muttered Mr Macavity. "Well, Saffy?"

"It's nothing to do with you," shouted Saffy. "And why are *you* here?"

Harry was feeling very, very sick!

"I have a prrrrresent for you, Saffy," Mr Macavity said and growled.

"I don't like your presents, Mr Macavity," retorted Saffy.

Mr Macavity laughed. And with a swish of his tail, he ran outside again. Saffy and Harry looked at each other, wondering what was going to happen next.

Then before they could shut the door, Mr Macavity ran back inside with a huge rat in his mouth! "*Urggh*," shrieked Saffy. She ran to the human washing place, heading for the toilet! Harry stared and stared at the rat. He had never seen one so big. He started to heave, just like when he had furballs!

Macavity snarled. "Worthless kitties, you and your Happeelix! You don't know what you are missing." he turned with a twitch of his tail and took the rat to the garden to eat in peace. He would be back to scare those kitties again. That's for sure!

13

The Magic Beanstalk

Magic, magic, little beans,
Let's grow the biggest stalk you've seen.
Magic, magic stairs of green,
Let's grow the biggest dream you've seen.
Magic steps up, one, two, three.
Come make a wish for you and me.
Two best friends; let us climb
into the clouds and wish sublime.
Magic cat, me by your side,
My whiskers for you, I cannot hide.
You make my sunshine on my fur,
You make my trembles and my purr.
Magic, magic, little beans,
Let's grow the biggest stalk you've seen.
Magic, magic stairs above,
Let's grow our wonderous tale of love.

Breakfast on day 5 of his stay was a grand affair with fishy fingers, biscuits, and ham. Harry felt very lucky and spoilt. He was settling down for a nap when Saffy proclaimed, "Harry, we must go up the beanstalk today."

What? Harry didn't know where the beanstalk was and where they would go. After the visit to the beefburgers, he thought they would rest and enjoy the squishy cushions. But no; Saffy wanted an adventure!

"Harry, there is a beanstalk in our garden glass house. Come on. I will show you."

Off they trotted across the grass and past the dinosaurs' house. The dinosaurs were still in their beds, but one of them called to Saffy, "Where are you going, Saffy? Can we come?"

"No, dinosaurs, you can't. We are going to a special place. We going to go up the beanstalk," replied Saffy.

Harry was nervous. He had never heard of a beanstalk, let alone climb one. What would it be like? Saffy seemed to like dangerous adventures!

Saffy took him into the glass house. Harry had seen one of these in his mummy's garden, but it wasn't like this! There were plants and flowers everywhere. The colours were beautiful. And the smells made his whiskers twitch excitedly. He wanted to explore this extraordinary place which was warm and cosy and full of light.

"Here, Harry, here it is! It's been growing for ages, and now it is huge," shrieked Saffy. And there on the shelf was what Saffy had been calling a beanstalk! It had long, fat, green leaves. There was a huge orange ball on the top of its very long stem. Harry wondered what they were supposed to do now.

"Look, Harry. We can climb up the beanstalk and sit on the orange cushion. Then we can make a wish and go anywhere we want," announced Saffy.

Harry thought about this for a little while. He wasn't sure where he wanted to go, apart from back to the cushions in Saffy's bedroom.

"Come on, Harry, come on." And with that, Saffy leaped onto the shelf and stretched up the beanstalk. The beanstalk swayed under her paws. *Crikey,* thought Harry, *this looks tricky!* Then Saffy jumped and sat on the orange ball. Then Saffy announced, "I wish we were at the beach." She shut her eyes tightly. Nothing happened! So she said her wish again. Still nothing happened! "I don't think it's working, Harry," she muttered. "Maybe it needs new batteries."

Harry didn't think it needed batteries, but he didn't like to say.

Saffy leapt down from the orange ball. "Come on, Harry, you have a go. It might work for you."

Harry gulped and jumped. He landed on the orange ball! It started to bend and sway quite precariously. "Uh, Saffy, this isn't right. It won't stay still."

"Never mind, Harry. It will be OK. Just make a wish!"

Harry wished he was back in the ground! He didn't like this orange ball moving about at all. Suddenly, the orange ball bent right over, and Harry slid to the ground!

"Harry, what's happening? Did you make a wish?"

Harry started to feel better. "Yes, Saffy, I made a wish!"

"What was it, Harry?"

"Saffy, I don't think you are meant to say what your wishes are, but I did wish to be back on the ground."

"Crikey, Harry, it works!" Saffy was thrilled.

"I don't think we should try it again, Saffy." He knew she was thinking that she would give it another go. "I think I used its battery up. We can try again tomorrow, if you like!"

"OK, Harry. That sounds like a good idea"

Phew, thought Harry. He had managed to avert a potential disaster.

"I think we should go and play mousey now, Harry," announced Saffy as she strutted down the garden to the house. Harry galloped after her, quite relieved that the beanstalk had not taken them away.

"Coming, Saffy," he said worth a purr. He was looking forward to a game of mousey!

14

The Mysterious Visitor

Harry awoke after an uneasy sleep. Several times in the night he felt his tail bristle, a sure sign that something wasn't right. He had sat in the tower in the lounge to see if he could see anyone there. He couldn't quite make out what was happening in the garden as there was no moonlight; and his eyes couldn't see if someone was moving about.

He had heard something though. And this was on top of the snoring coming from Saffy and her mummy!

He stretched himself, trying to galvanise himself into action. His nose twitched, and his tail flicked in anticipation. He ran down the corridor from the bedroom to the lounge and jumped up on the tower.

Good grief! What had happened to the lawn. It was covered in huge lumps of earth! They made a pattern on the grass that went right up to the small house.

Harry jumped down from the tower and ran to find Saffy. They had to investigate this. Saffy had heard Harry running about and had jumped down from the blanket tower.

"Saffy, Saffy, come and look at what has happened in the garden! It happened last night. I am sure of it," blurted Harry. "Something has invaded the garden."

Saffy looked out of the window and saw the lumps on the lawn. "Oh, crikey, Harry. Let's go and see what they are!"

They both gingerly went down and out of the patio doors, up the steps past the lavender, and on to the lawn. They stopped at the first lump and sniffed it. Nothing to smell apart from earth. They repeated this at every lump. But when they got to the second from the last lump, something smelled different. And they could feel something move under the earth. Saffy started to dance around excitedly, her tail waving in the air. "Harry, Harry, something is here. I know it is! Put your paw on it, Harry, and see what happens!"

Thanks, Saffy, thought Harry. *I get all the good jobs!* He patted the lump of earth with his paw. It felt soft and dry. He prodded it again, and this time it moved! Then a nose appeared!

"What?" Then Saffy screamed. "What?"

"Well, hello there, "came a low, soft, velvety voice. And suddenly, the rest of the animal appeared. Its soft velvety voice matched its soft, brown, velvety body. Small beady eyes peered at Harry and Saffy, inquisitive and soul searching.

"Is that you, Harry and Saffy?"

Harry and Saffy were stunned! This creature knew their names. How?

Saffy remembered her manners and stopped gawking at the creature. "I am terribly sorry", she apologized, "but we don't know who or what you are. And how do you know our names?"

"Ah," replied that rich, velvety voice. "Do excuse me. I shall introduce myself. I am Professor Maurice Mole."

"Well, hello, Professor Maurice Mole," schmoozed Saffy. She was quite delighted with his velvety voice. "You are very welcome here, but why are you here, and how do you know us?"

"Well, my lady Saffy, I know you from your box footprint, your spiders web activity, and from your adventures with the orange ball in the glass house," replied the professor. "I am here because I need to talk to you both about something very secret indeed!"

"Oh, come on, Saffy, "said Harry. He wasn't sure about this creature at all, with his smooth ways and smooth coat. He noted that Saffy was quite transfixed with this Professor Mole, but Harry thought there was something quite dangerous about him.

"No, no, Harry. Let's hear what the professor has to say." Saffy was getting curiouser and curiouser by the minute. She started to dance around, and her tail swirled. Her yellow eyes grew in size and brightness.

"Harry, you are right to be cautious," assured Professor Mole. "I am from a very secret organisation, the NCA—the National Cats Agency. We fight organised crime. We work everywhere!"

"But why are you talking to us?" asked Harry. "Surely you don't think *we* are criminals." Harry winced, thinking of the times he snatched bees and baby birds to play with. *Would that make me a criminal?* Then there was that grass snake a couple summers ago. He played with that until its tail snapped off. That could be an even worse crime.

"No, Harry. We would like you to visit us and talk about the future," responded the mole. "You need to come to Catte Street in Oxfordian Town in two days' time. Be there at 10 o'clock in the morning. You will see a sign for Saint Gertrude's College. Go through the door, and someone will meet you. His tail will twitch three times, so you will know he is trusted."

Professor Maurice Mole handed Harry a small flat box tied with brown string. Harry caught the string in his claw and held it in front of his whiskers, examining more strange smells.

"Agent Harry and Detective Saffy, before you arrive, please get yourselves acquainted with the contents of this box. I cannot tell you what it is or what you need to do with it, but you are our top prospects for the future of the NCA. And we are certain you will work it out. This will be required to gain access to Saint Gertrude's College."

With that, Professor Maurice Mole was gone! Harry and Saffy stared at each other in amazement. What the whiskers was going to happen next?

15

The Openings

Agent Harry and Detective Saffy almost fell over themselves with excitement to get indoors. They galloped across the lawn and down the three steps and past the bumblebee lavender place. Harry was so excited that he did all three steps in one leap and landed nose-first into the patio doors!

"Saffy, wait for me! Where are you?"

"Harry, come on! I'm in my secret place, where I take my treasures."

Harry and Saffy ran into her mummy's bedroom and then into the human washing place. Harry watched her sleek little tail disappear underground. Where the whiskers did she go?

Harry peered down and saw a little hole behind the steps to the human washing place! There was his little Saffy sausage!

He jumped down through the cobwebs, and Saffy was in her little den. She had lit a little candle. Harry laughed when he saw the stash of Happeelix, a piece of string, a toilet roll, a nail file, and a long piece of purple ribbon that Saffy had hidden in her treasure hole.

"Come on, Harry, let's open it together!"

Harry looked at Saffy's beautiful face. Her eyes were as big and round as the moon. They were deep black with a hint of mischief and the most stunning yellow hues. "Saffy, why did your mummy call you that name?"

"It's short for Saffron, Harry. My mummy chose it because she said my eyes are like the spice or something. I don't know what she's on about. I just purr and let her think she is very clever!"

Harry and Saffy each took an end of the string. They gently pulled their ends, and the box popped open! Saffy flipped the lid off.

"What the flipping whiskers is that?" asked Harry. "Saffy, I knew this was a bad idea and we that we should not trust the moley man. He is a spy. We will never know what to do with this. What is it? Why is? What have we done? What is it for?"

"Harry, you need to calm down. You always do this. Just put your tail back in its box. I, Detective Saffy Smart, know *exactly* what this is! Ha!"

Harry was so pleased that Saffy was his best friend. She was quite the pussy cat! If he was to be Harry Bond, then she would be his Pussy Galore!

"Right, Harry. I've seen Daddy Nick teaching this to my mummy. I'm so, so, so excited. I watched them do the game, and I know how to do it! We just need a door to practice on!"

Harry looked again. How was this a game? In the box were eight metal sticks. What on earth was it for? All the sticks were silver; all were the same length and width. Some had wiggly ends, some had pointy ends, and some had flat ends. One looked a bit different from the others. Saffy called that one the "wiggler".

The winning Wiggle stick

Saffy picked the sticks up in her teeth and ran like a horsey. She flicked her tail in Harry's face, and he got a mouth full of the furry bed monsters and a cobweb! *Saffy is lucky she is beautiful and clever,* he thought.

Saffy had gone into the far bedroom place and into a big cupboard, where she sat looking through the little lock hole. "Right, Harry. Pick a stick, any stick, and put it in the lockey thing. I will put the wiggler in, and we will jiggle them around. Then we will see if we can open the door!"

"Don't be silly, Saffy. That's ridiculous. You cannot break into a door with two sticks. You are mad! I don't want to do it. It's not fun anymore, and I don't want to go to Oxfordian Town. You can take Mr Macavity instead."

"Harry, for frog sakes! Just cat up, will you? Right, first stick … and wiggle. Nope! Next one."

One by one, Harry and Saffy tried the wiggle sticks. When they got to the fifth one, which was shaped like a wiggly worm with a hook on the end, *Pop!* The door swung open.

Harry almost fell on his whiskers! "Saffy, we did it. We are special catnapper agents!"

"Teamwork makes the dream work, Harry!"

Harry stared at Saffy. She really was a wonder!

"What, Harry? What's the matter?" Saffy purred. She knew he thought she was great; she could tell! *Nothing wrong with that,* she thought. *May it long continue!*

She was my best friend. ♡

"Come on, Harry. Let's go back to the secret hole and hide the wigglers. We need to keep them safe. We don't want anyone else to find them before we go Oxfordian Town"

So they went returned to the secret hole and put the wigglers back in the special box. Harry looked around him. Saffy had collected so many different things, and he wasn't sure why.

"Saffy, why is there a toilet roll in here? What is so special about that?"

"You can do all kinds of things with toilet roll, Harry. You can write secret messages on it, you can use it as a bandage if you hurt yourself, and it can be a slide rope to escape out of windows. Or you can trap hoomans with it by running it all around their feet! Mostly, Harry, I like to play football with it!"

Crikey, thought Harry, *I would never have imagined that. That's why they want Saffy as a detective; she knows so much already.* "And the purple ribbon, Saffy, what do you do with that?"

"I dance with that, Harry. I spin around with it wrapped around my tail. It can make creatures dizzy and fall over! Or they fall in love with me!"

Oh, heck. Harry sighed. *Here we go again.* First it was Mr Macavity, and now it was the purple ribbon making Harry's green eyes go greener. He noticed on the wood burner thingy that he and Saffy were not the only pawtraits he had seen. Who were they all? If he wasn't careful, he would be turned into green-eyed monster. He would have to learn to control himself, or he would get into trouble.

Harry decided he would ask about the nail file and the string another time. He was quite hungry from all the excitement. "Saffy, can we eat the Happeelix please. Or do you have any ham snax? I'm starving."

"Harry, we should have some proper fud. Let's go and see what Mummy has made us this morning."

So out of the secret hole they came into the human washing place. They went down the long corridor, playing horsey as they went. They were so excited. They raced into the kitchen, almost tripping over each other's tails until they came to the fud bowls.

Saffy's mummy had filled them up with tuna and tiny biscuits. Harry stuck his head in the bowl and stuffed his face. Saffy delicately nibbled at her tuna. Harry eventually surfaced from his fud, tuna juice dripping off his whiskers and chin. "Urgh, Harry, your whiskers are disgusting! Quick, lick them up, please!" Harry snorted and licked his whiskers, enjoying his second round of tuna!

"Saffy, have you thought about how we will get to Oxfordian Town?" Harry didn't have a clue what to do. "Maybe we could ask your mummy to take us in the Pawschee."

"No, Harry. I won't go in the Pawschee. It makes me sick and scared! Besides, I don't think it's a good idea for mummy to know where we are going. She will want to know what we are doing, and we *can't* tell her. I have heard about the giant electric caterpillars, Harry. We could travel by caterpillar to Oxfordian Town and then use a catnav to find Catte Street."

"Saffy, we will look on the box to see about the caterpillars." So off went. They jumped on the table to check the box. But Harry was beginning to wonder if Saffy was a cat biscuit short of a box. Giant caterpillars? Whatever.

In their excitement, the detective duo hadn't noticed Mr Macavity by the open door. He had been listening to everything they said! He slinked off into the bushes, smiling to himself.

16

The Great Journey

Saffy had been on the box for ages. Harry watched her pawing madly at the keys and looking closely at the screen. "What can I do, Saffy?" Shall I pack some Happeelix for the journey?"

"No, Harry, I wouldn't do that. "Could you go and ask the beefburgers when the tractor will go past the HiddeyHole and Tail Station tomorrow to catch the giant electric caterpillars? We need to get to HiddeyHole by nine o'clock in the morning."

Saffy continued on the box as Harry slipped out of the door and past the lumps in the lawn. *What a mess,* he thought. He wandered on down the lane to find the beefburgers. It was a cool day. A slight mist covered the fields and made Harry's fur tingle. *I think this can be a spooky place.* He didn't know why? He just had a feeling.

He saw the beefburgers in the distance and crossed the muddy fields to reach them. *Good thing Saffy isn't here. She would be up to her tufty ears in mud!* He grinned when he remembered how she got stuck in the mud and was so cross when she had to have a bath!

"Hello, Harry," rumbled Bert as Harry approached. "How are you and that sassy Saffy doing today?"

Harry nearly blurted out that they had met Professor Mole, but he stopped himself just in time. "We are doing fine, Bert. Thank you. Hope you are too? No sign of the freezer yet?"

"No, Harry," replied Bert with a glint in his eye. "I am a freezer dodger, you know!"

Harry didn't know why, but he thought Bert was always right about things in life. So he decided to ask him outright. "Bert, Saffy asked me to ask you when the tractor will be coming past here tomorrow as we need to get to HiddeyHole and Tail Station by nine o'clock in the morning."

Bert frowned and thought for a while. "I think you will have to get up every early, Harry, as it takes a while to get to HiddeyHole on the tractor. Then you need to walk from the fields to get on the caterpillar."

Harry gulped. Saffy wasn't good at getting up early, and she would be grumpy for sure!

"Be at the bottom of this lane by eight o'clock tomorrow morning, Harry, be sure to take a seafurball tablet as it's very rocky on the tractor."

That sounds exciting, thought Harry. He would have to see if Saffy had any seafurball tablets as he had no doubt that she wouldn't do "rocky".

"Thank you, Bert," replied Harry. "That's really helpful. And keep dodging the freezer!" With that, Harry ran over the fields and back to the farm to tell Saffy the news. The mist was clearing now, and the sun had appeared. Harry could see drainage ditches at the side of the field. His sharp eyes picked out movement. *Rats!* He could make out their long, greasy, shiny tails in the sunlight. He shuddered. He *hated* rats. They were miserable and mean, in his opinion. He had never heard of a nice rat.

Harry hurried on, not wanting the rats to spot him. But he *had* been spotted by Macavity.

What's Hopeless Harry up to? wondered Macavity. *He really is clueless. No need to worry about him finding anything out. But Saffy is another matter.* He knew she was sharp as claws, and he would have to deal with her in time. His black raisin eyes narrowed as he watched Harry head for the kitchen. He would have to listen at the doors again he. Something was definitely apaw. He limped back into the bushes, dragging his wonky tail behind him, and sat and hummed to himself.

Harry raced into the kitchen with his slightly muddy paws making patterns on the creamy floor. He was just about to sit on the cream cocktail chair when Saffy screeched at him, "Putrid paws, Harry. Putrid paws!"

"What?" yowled Harry.

"Your paws are putrid, Harry, from the mud. You must go and clean them immediately."

Harry shook his ears. His emerald-green eyes widened in amazement. He wondered if Saffy really wanted to hear his news at all. This was urgent. He didn't have time to clean his paws!

"You can't leave traces of mud, Harry, Mummy will wonder what we've been up to and where we have been. If we are going to be spies, Harry, we have to become invisible!"

Harry let Saffy carry on for a while and then muttered, "Eight o'clock, Saffy. The tractor, end of the road, we need seafurball tablets."

Saffy stopped chiding Harry and sat bolt upright! "That's rather early, Harry! And I haven't got any seafurball tablets."

"Bert said it was going to be a rocky ride on the tractor, Saffy. He advised us to have some seafurball tablets ready," Harry explained.

"Well, we will just have to brave Harry. I think it's too late to get the seafurball stuff. Anyway, did anyone see you talking to the beefburgers?"

"I saw some rats in the ditches, Saffy. But I didn't see anyone else. At least not that I noticed."

Saffy purred to herself. They were going to have such an exciting time. She had worked out from the box the way to St Gertrude's, and she felt very proud of herself!

Bert had been right. The tractor was indeed bumpy as it made its way over the misty fields. Harry tried to see where they were heading, but it was so grey and grizzly it was hard to see much on the horizon.

The tractor had arrived at the bottom of the road, just as Bert had advised. Harry and Saffy jumped into the cabin via the huge wheels. It was a tricky task as the tyres were slippery from the mud. They had to claw their way up. Once inside the cabin, the driver nodded to them. He was a strange sight. He had a long, brown, shaggy beard, and piercing brown eyes behind round tortoise-shell glasses. He wore a long brown coat. Saffy noticed he had pieces of wood tied to his shoes so he could reach the tractor's peddles. In some way, he reminded Saffy of Professor Mole. *He must be quite small*, Saffy thought. "Can you take us to HiddeyHole and Tail Station, please?"

"Of course. Bert said that's where you want to go. We are on our way," replied Macgrumpy.

Then they were off across the fields, bumping along over the ridges of the earth. *Thud, thud, thud* Harry's and Saffy's bottoms went on the hard red seats. *I hope this doesn't take too long,* Harry thought. *I think this will wear all my fur off!*

Thirty minutes passed, which seemed an awfully long time to Harry. Then the Tractor slowed down. A long track appeared, and a low building surrounded by blue railings was in front of them.

"That's where you need to be," said Macgrumpy, pointing to the low building. "You need to go across this last bit of field, through the railings, and then you can get on the caterpillar. Be careful to watch for the electric doors to open, and then you can jump on! Mind yourselves. I will see you both later."

Harry and Saffy clawed themselves down the muddy tyres and made their way across the field to the railings. They squeezed their bodies through the railings and sat on the platform.

"I have never been on an electric caterpillar. Have you, Saffy?" asked a nervous Harry. His whiskers and tail twitched nervously.

"No, I haven't, Harry. But I have seen them on the box, and they look very nice! I think we will be fine. The journey isn't a long one, and I have it all worked out." Saffy excitedly twitched her tail and nose. Her yellow eyes glowed!

At that moment, a long, blue, giant, electric caterpillar glided towards them. "It's the caterpillar, Harry. It's the caterpillar," shouted Saffy.

The caterpillar stopped, and with a *wooooshing* sound, the doors opened on the side of the caterpillar. Hoomans seemed to come out from nowhere and get on the train. "Quick, Harry. We *must* get on the caterpillar! If we don't get on, then we won't get to St Gertrude's. Jump, Harry, jump," shouted Saffy.

They both leapt into the caterpillar as the doors closed, *woosh!* They were in the blue shiny tube. They dodged the hooman feet and bags and found a quiet corner to curl up in. "Harry, this feels like moving in the Pawschee, it's going so fast," cried Saffy. "I am not sure I like it too much!"

"It will be OK, Saffy. Just curl up, and I will watch over you," Harry comforted Saffy.

They heard the hooman shout out strange names of places that they didn't know as they travelled along. Harry wondered how much longer it would be before they could get off and in to the fresh air. Saffy was still curled up tightly when they heard the hooman say over the shouty caterpillar, "Next stop is Oxfordian Town. All change. All change, please. Last stop on this service."

Saffy unwound herself, stretched her long, supple body, and flexed her claws. "This is where we get off, Harry. It's Oxfordian Town." She was feeling stronger now that she knew their journey on the caterpillar was coming to an end.

The green electric caterpillar drew into the station at Oxfordian Town, and its doors opened. Harry and Saffy jumped off before all the hoomans. But they were stopped in their pawtracks. This station was supersized! Hoomans and more hoomans criss-crossed each other's paths as they ran for other tubes or to get out of the station. Bags and umbrellas swung in their way, almost taking off Saffy's and Harry's noses and whiskers!

"I think we should wait until it's a bit quieter. What do you think, Harry?"

"Good idea, Saffy." So they sat behind a big, red post box in the hall of the station. After a short while, the station had emptied of hoomans.

Saffy suddenly gasped. "Harry!"

"What, Saffy?"

"The wigglers! Do you got the wigglers? I haven't got them!"

"Don't worry, Saffy. I have them here in my little black bag." Sure enough, as Harry turned round, Saffy caught sight of a little black bag hidden in Harry's fur. "You don't think I would forget them, do you? I wouldn't be much of an agent if I had, would I?" Harry laughed.

"Sorry, Harry. Having to get up early in the morning is soooo hard. I would have forgotten my tail if it wasn't attached, you know!" She sighed.

"So Saffy, do you know which way it is to St Gertrude's? Will it take us long to get there?"

"Oh, yes, Harry. That is why I was so long on the box. I looked at the maps, and I have the way to go in my head. It will take us about twenty ticktocks to get there, which is like three mealtimes!"

Harry gasped. "That's quite a long time, Saffy."

"It will go quickly. Don't worry, Harry." And with that, they left the caterpillar place. They zigzagged along the streets and dodged the hoomans' shoes. They arrived at a road full of cars, buses, and bicycles. They both gasped and walked close to the back of the pavement, where they felt safe away from the noise and smells. Suddenly, Harry heard something very different. It was water! They were running over a bridge with a river below them, Harry stopped and looked through the blue railings, wondering whether there was any fish to be found.

"Don't stop, Harry! We can't be late. Hurry, hurry," Saffy called as she ran ahead. They carried on up the long road. "This is George Street, Harry," stated Saffy.

"I had a friend called George," reminisced Harry. But Saffy wasn't listening. She was hurrying up the road.

Harry suddenly stopped and called Saffy back. "Look, Saffy. Look at this." Harry stared into the Old Fire House Gallery window, where he could see wonderful, colourful pictures of cats. "Your mummy makes pictures like this, doesn't she, Saffy? I have seen them in your house."

Saffy rushed back to look. "You are right, Harry. They *are* Mummy's pictures! She is famous, I think! But we can't stop now. Come on." Harry wanted to linger by the pictures. They felt familiar to him and made him want to purr, but Saffy was moving quickly, and he had to keep up.

They rushed to Broady Street. Harry noticed that it was full of bookshops. The smells from the open doors were different and intriguing. Then it was Saffy's turn to stop.

"Harry, we are nearly here. That is the Catleian Library, a very famous book place, you know. I think St Gertrude's College is just around the corner." Harry didn't want to tell Saffy he didn't know what a library was. He would find out what it was.

They turned the corner onto Catte Street. They found a huge wooden door with a picture of a cat above the archway. They stared hard at the door. Were they in the right place? Then Saffy saw the sign: "St Gertrude's College.

As they got closer to the door, they realised there was I small panel in the huge door, like a cat flap, in the bottom right-hand side. "I think this is where we use the wigglers, Harry," said Saffy as she peered at the small panel. Harry got the wigglers out of his bag, and Saffy set to work opening the panel. Suddenly the panel opened, and they could go into the college. They jumped through the panel and were immediately in the path of a silver-coloured cat.

He was a young cat with bright yellow eyes and a kind face. He smiled shyly. Then he turned round and twitched his huge tail three times. This was just as Professor Maurice Mole had said would happen.

Harry and Saffy followed the silver cat around the edge of the quadrangle and then across the lawn. *No lumps in this lawn,* thought Harry!. Then they went up a narrow spiral staircase with stone steps. Up and up they went, round and round. It made Harry's head spin going up and around so many times!

"Harry, this is amazing!" whispered Saffy. "I love it here. I think it's so exciting!"

The silver cat beckoned to them to hurry. They looked at each other, their whiskers twitched in unison, and they quickened their paws. The silver cat ran ahead and came to a stop outside another wooden door. This time he pushed it open with his paw, and Saffy and Harry saw a wonderful sight!

The room was panelled in wood, and cat portraits hung all around the room. There were long tables with very tall chairs positioned next to them. Saffy counted ten chairs pulled out with red cushions placed on top of them. She wondered why there were only ten cushions when there were so many seats.

Then she looked around the room and saw eight cats sitting bolt upright, patiently looking up at Professor Maurice Mole, who sat at a table on a platform at the front of the room. "Harry, Harry, we are here. We are at *spy school.*" Harry's tail quivered in anticipation. They were indeed here. He wondered what on earth would happen next.

17

Spy School

Professor Mole drew himself up to his full height. His velvet coat gleamed and his eyes sparkled behind his strange monocle. "Welcome, my young friends. Thank you for coming here today. I know some of you have travelled long and difficult journeys to get here. It is so important that you are here. You are the chosen ones!"

The cats twitched their tails in excitement. Some even rolled around in eager anticipation. Saffy looked around, keen to see who else was there. Would she know anyone? She didn't think so, but you never know. She saw a wonderful array of colours and sizes of cats: smooth dark-grey, fluffy medium-grey, tortoise shell, foxy orange, silver grey, and palomino. Saffy

"Before we do a paw call, I will explain to you all why you are here. Some of you may have looked up the NCA on your boxes and seen the work we do. If you haven't, then I shall tell you. The NCA is *the* leading cat intelligence service in England. We fight organised crime in the animal world. Sometimes these crimes span countries. Sometimes it happens in our own backyards, so to speak. Cat agencies around the world contact us to help them with their crimes.

"Today", he continued without pausing for breath, "is your first day of spy school. You will learn our pawcraft. Some of which you will remember immediately. Other lessons will need to be practiced. I promise you it will be exciting! Spy school will teach you how to disguise yourself, how to make secret messages, and how to carry out pawveillance."

"I want you all to introduce yourselves to the group now. Keep it short and sweet." The professor sat on a plump cushion and puffed. He straightened his monocle and reached for an earthworm from his plate next to the cushion.

The kitties all looked at each other with wide eyes, wondering who would speak first. Saffy decided she would go first. She stretched, flexed her claws, and opened her yellow eyes wide. "I am Saffy Smart, and I live on a farm with my mummy. And I love partying!"

Crikey, Harry thought, *what can I say?* He decided he would let someone else go ahead of him.

The silver cat who led them to the schoolroom coughed. Then in a very quiet meow, said, "I am Louis. I love hiding in secret places and climbing trees!" He sat back down quickly and curled his long fluffy tail around his body.

Next to announce themselves was a very sleek grey cat with bright-green slit eyes. With a sharp hiss, she proclaimed, "I am Edie. I will say no more!" And with that, she sat bolt upright, her head in the air.

Luna, an extremely fluffy grey cat with white fluffy socks and a white fluffy bowtie on her tummy, pounced forward with a shriek and a giggle. "Hee, hee, I am Luna. I am the sister of Louis, but he never tells anyone that." Then she giggled again and rolled her golden eyes. Luna rolled over and over on the wooden floor. *More like Luna the lunatic*, thought Harry.

little luna♡

Harry decided to speak up, and he sat up straight. He opened his green eyes wide and then narrowed them. Pointing his ears forward, he introduced himself. "I am Harry. I live far from here, with the dirties. And my best friend is Saffy." He was going to continue but remembered that the professor had instructed them to be brief. So he stopped abruptly. He looked down and to the side to see if anyone had been listening to him. He realised that they all had! Professor Mole nodded at him as if to reassure Harry that it was all OK.

A tiny palomino kitty sat up quickly. She had orange, black, and white patches all over her, bright sparkly eyes and a cheeky smile. "I am Fifi," she announced. "I am so excited to be here. I love the box and exploring!" She looked towards Saffy to see if she could make a connection. Saffy looked at her out of the corner of her eye. *Mmmm, the jury is out on that one*, thought

Harry. But he thought Saffy and Fifi they would become friends. There was something about Fifi that Harry quite liked.

Next, a tall and sleek cat, who was almost the spitting image of Saffy, meowed. With her bright eyes and a real growl, she was sexy, but Harry could tell she could be a real Bristolian street brawler. "My name is Gina; my mummy is Jodie. My best friend is Tilly Grace Castle. She pulls my fur, my tail, and my ears. And I don't mind. But anyone else …" Gina purred. Harry thought his luck was in—*two of Saffy!*

meeoowww!

A very loud purr came from Harry's right. He looked to see a beautiful, tall, and gentle cat. "Hello, everyone. My name is Stella. I'm twenty-two hooman years, and my right leg looks like the stripes of a caramel-chocolate nougat bar." Stella was the most beautiful mix of browns and golden hues, with a white tummy and stripey, chocolate, tiger legs.

Mabel, an empress amongst cats—at least that's how she considered herself—stretched herself out before she announced herself. She was a very haughty tortie. She had a small M on her forehead in black fur. "I am Mabel," she proclaimed. "I was a model when I was younger. I posed as the world's most beautiful kitten. I gave all that up as I found all the adulation rather boring!" Mabel deployed a death stare at all the kitties in case anyone dared to challenge her. "The other information that you need to know is that I am immortal!"

Harry thought she had the most beautiful tortoiseshell markings, and her green eyes were most expressive. She had dreadlocks and a beautiful white ruff. *Crikey,* thought Harry, *she is a boss cat!*

The last cat to introduce himself was a small black and white boy. "My full name is Forest Teriyaki McTwittle, the Thane of Felinnnne. I have a large ancestral estate on the Firth of Felinnnne, just north of Moray. You can call me Twittle for short!" Forest spoke with a strong Scottish accent. He continued, "I often go the KitKat Club in Brightown with my brother, Marcel. You can find us there drinking mousee on Friday nights." Forest was very jolly and had a twinkle in his eye. Harry liked the look of him. Harry noticed that Saffy certainly liked the look of him. That made Harry's green eyes flare!

With all the introductions complete, the mole stood. He had a little bit of worm hanging off his whiskers, but no one dared say anything about it.

"Thank you, everyone. Now we will start to learn our pawcraft. You will need to listen very carefully. And don't forget that you can't write anything down. Please take your seats."

All the kitties ran to the long table and jumped onto the red cushions. Saffy looked at Harry and grinned. "This is going to be *exciting*. I can't wait! Do you think we will be long? Mummy might get worried if we are gone too long!"

"Shush, Saffy. We must listen to the professor," whispered Harry. "We don't want to get in trouble!"

Professor Mole began the lesson. "You will see that each one of you have a bag in front of you. Inside you will find the secret box, some fur dye, some very special Happeelix, and a smoke bombee! These are pawcraft."

Harry and Saffy looked inside their bags. The secret box was a very tiny version of the box Saffy had at home. "You will conceal the secret box in your fur, behind your ear. Please try this now."

The kitties tried to put their secret boxes behind their ears. For some, it was very difficult. "I can't make it stay there, sir," cried Fifi.

"Lick your paw, and then lick the secret box. Then it should stay there," advised the professor. And sure enough, it did when Fifi followed his advice.

"Your secret box is how you talk to your fellow agents. You will see that it glows when you put your paw on it. It has the numbers of the agents stored inside. But you can only make calls when it is an emergency!"

"You can send secret messages using the invisible ink feature on the secret box. You write your messages like normal pawscibing. And when someone receives, it will look like a blank message. Only the recipient can read it when they put their paw on the screen and slide their paw across the text! Try this now!"

Suddenly, the secret box in front of Saffy pinged and glowed pink. "Harry, Harry, I have a message," squealed Saffy. She put her paw on the screen and slid it across. An image started to appear of Fifi dancing and swirling her tail, and it spoke, "Will you be my friend, Saffy?" Then it purred. Saffy gasped in surprise and amazement. "Harry, look at this. It's amazing!"

Harry was too busy trying to work out how to send his message. He had decided to send a message to Forest, but he worried because his spelling wasn't very good. He wrote, "helo Forest, it's gud to meat you!"

Saffy saw what he was doing and corrected him. "Use the kitty check button on the box, Harry," she advised. Harry pushed the button, and lo and behold, the words changed. The message was sent! Forest jumped in the air when his box pinged and glowed purple.

All around the table the secret boxes pinged and glowed. "Good! I think you have all got the hang of that technique," commented the professor. "There is another invisible ink technique that you need to learn. In your bag is a small blue bottle. Use this ink on any paper to paw a message, and then carefully fold the paper like this." The professor demonstrated by taking a small piece of paper and carefully folding it into the shape of a bird, which then actually flew off!

The little bird landed in front of Luna, who giggled and stared at it. "Pick it up with your claw, and purr on it, Luna," the professor said. Luna stared at the little bird and purred *very* loudly. Then she giggled again. The little bird opened up, and Luna saw the message inside: "Congratulations, Luna."

Everyone gasped in awe. This was magic! Everyone wanted to make a bird right away, but the professor was keen to press on. "You will all need to learn code for the messages, but not today. That will be your homework from a code book that will be in the special box.

"You will see that you all have fur dye in your bags. This is to be used very carefully. It will not stay in your fur long. You can make stripes or circles on your fur, dip your paws in it, or the ends of your ears. This will change your appearance. Practice this at home when the hoomans aren't around. Please note if you are black, your fur dye will appear white.

"You will see there is a special packet of Happeelix in your bag. A few drops of this special Happeelix will immediately send any creature to sleep for one hour. You only need to use a few drops. Then you can contact NCA using your special boxes, and we will dispose of the creature for you. It is very important please to remember that it lasts for sixty minutes *exactly*. No longer.

"Our pawcraft requires us all to learn purveillance. You all need to assume that you are being watched at all times. It doesn't mean to say that someone is following behind you as you walk outside. But we can all be watched from eyes in the sky or from jelliwobblers as they hover above us. Your special boxes may have buggels in them, and the bad uns can be listening to you. You need to be focussed and use your great peripheral vision. All kitties have a wide field of view; this is what we call peripheral vision. Y have probably noticed it when you suddenly see an unwanted hooman approaching you from the side or a mousey wriggling in the corner. This vision will help you spot anyone watching you.

"When you spot someone watching you, don't look back at them as this makes you look like you are nervous. Just keep walking with your tail and whiskers high in the air. Remember, it could be anyone watching. It could be a dragonfly mouse, a one-eyed frog, or an old grey beard.

"And remember this next step in your pawcraft: Never walk three sides of a square. If you do, you might bump into one of your followers. To keep a low profile, never turn left twice in a row. This gives you away and blows your cover. You need to learn to cross the road carefully, making a turn as you go. This way you can check to see if anyone is behind you without looking directly behind you."

Crikey, thought Harry. *There is a lot to remember here.* He wasn't even sure if he had ever been in a square. He would ask Saffy; she would know. He noticed that Saffy was busy tip-tapping on her secret box. *Is she taking notes?* he wondered.

Harry was jolted out of his thoughts as Professor Mole announced, "Never run!" *What?* thought Harry. *What kind of advice is that?.* He and Saffy ran everywhere! They played horsey in Saffy's house and ran after the bumblebees in the garden! "When you think you have been spotted by another agent, never run," continued the professor. "It will break your cover as an agent."

Phew, that's OK then, thought Harry. He had wondered how he would play with Saffy if he never ran.

"And lastly, my cat agents, the smoke bombee. This little round ball will give you cover to escape dangerous situations. Just extend a claw into the soft, round ball, and smoke will appear that will confuse your enemies, allowing you to escape."

Professor Mole moved around his platform, looking thoughtful. He noticed the kitties had started to flick their tales and twitch their whiskers. *Hmmm,* he thought, *maybe it's time for a break. They need their Happeelix fixe*s.

"So, my new recruits, I need to give you your first take today." The professor's voice turned velvety, and his tiny eyes narrowed even further. "But first, we will have some Happeelix to keep us focussed. Then I will tell you about an organisation known as the Vulpes Syndicate."

Suddenly, young ferrets delivered packets of Happeelix to the table. The ferrets looked around at the collection of kitties and nodded to each other. "Newbies," muttered one of the ferrets.

"Hmm. Wonder how many of those will last?" said another ferret. They snorted to each other.

The kitties tucked into the Happeelix with glee, purring as they went along. Harry looked at Saffy. Harry thought she seemed very excited. She was licking up the Happeelix eagerly and looking around at all the kitties in a very excited manner. Her lovely black tail swished, her eyes twitched, and her beautiful golden eyes widened.

"Harry, what do you think a take is?" asked Saffy. "And who is the Vulpes Syndicate? I wonder if they are anywhere near our house?"

Harry was starting to feel a little nervous. What if Macavity was one of these bad-uns. He thought he may well be. He certainly wasn't a good-un!

18

The Vulpes Syndicate

After all the kitties finished their Happeelix and the ferrets had removed all the bowls, Professor Mole stood at the edge of his platform, staring purposefully at his pupils. His snout twitched as he pushed his monocle up.

"OK, agents, I am going to tell you something top secret now. You must not speak of what I am going to tell you to anyone unless I ask you to! I introduce you to the Vulpe Syndicate. This syndicate is responsible for carrying out counter-intelligence, terrorism, revenge, and extortion all over the world. The global leader of the Vulpes Syndicate goes by the name of One-Eye Sly Fernandez. He runs his headquarters out of Spainland."

Professor Mole clicked his special box, and a screen dropped down behind him on which a large picture of One-Eye Sly Fernandez appeared on a map of Spainland, along with pictures of a large castle. One-Eye Sly looked very scary to Harry. He was a fox with one ear and a patch over one eye. He stood tall and proud with his big bushy tail that had a kink in it.

"He has run the syndicate since a young age. His father died, and he inherited this underworld," continued the professor. "He lost his eye fighting the wolves of Russialand during paw-to-paw combat. They were fighting over land and blood diamonds. The wolves captured him, cut off his ear, and broke his tail so that he was distinguishable by anyone in the know. The wolves let him go as a message to all those in the Vulpes Syndicate that this was what the wolves would do to them if they were caught in Russialand. One-Eye Sly travelled home by getting on a train at Alexandrovsky and travelling to Lviv before getting the bus to Madridy. He is crafty and clever and runs Vulpe from his palace in Granadaland.

"The Vulpe Syndicate has cells in every country in the world. Each fox looks different, so you need to go to the Catelonian Library and research and remember their appearances, habits, and where they all live.

"We are very interested in the Fennec Cell of the Vulpes Syndicate. It is based in Egyptland, and we know they are in contact with the English Red Cell.

"one eye"
SLY!!!

"The Vulpes Syndicate work closely with rattus rattus. Some of you will know of the rattus. They live in our towns and countrysides. They are everywhere!" The professor paused to wipe the beads of sweat from his brow. He had become quite animated briefing the kitties, pacing up and down and waving his special box around as he spoke. He took a gulp of air and continued. "The Vulpe Syndicate exploit, steal, and blackmail our countrymen and other good-uns around the world so that they can buy their most loved treasure—blood diamonds! These blood diamonds are stockpiled to fund their future illegal activities. Our job is to break up all the syndicate cells to stop them from acquiring more blood diamonds. And to take back the already stolen blood diamonds, of course."

Saffy felt that she had to speak. She stood up, and with her tail straight in the air, she asked, "Please, Professor, can you explain what are blood diamonds? I have never heard of them. What do they look like?"

"Well, Saffy, it's good that you ask these questions. Blood diamonds can be traced from the year 1989, which is a very long time ago in cat years. Blood diamonds are shiny beautiful jewels, but they are illegally mined in a country called Affricatt. Affricatt is facing a very bad situation of prolonged rebellion amongst foxes and cats. Obtaining blood diamonds is the primary purpose of their mining, and the jewels fund illegal activities which include buying guns and ammunition to oppose the rules and regulations of governments. The cats who have to collect these diamonds are very cruelly treated and live in terrible conditions. Sometimes even kittens are used to collect the diamonds because they are small enough to fit down the little hole mines! The demand and supply for blood diamonds must be stopped, Saffy."

All the kitties gasped as the professor clicked his special box, and pictures appeared of kittens in terrible conditions being made to go down the mines.

"Harry, we have to stop this, don't we?" whispered Saffy. "It's truly terrible!"

"I agree, Saffy. But how on earth are we going to do that?"

"Don't worry, Harry. We will learn how to do it. I am sure," Saffy said confidently.

The professor clicked his special box again, and this time a map appeared. Harry's and Saffy's eyes widened and nearly popped out of their heads. The map showed Saffy's farm and the fields they had walked in. It showed the next-door neighbours' gardens and the sheds at the back of the farm.

"Whattttttt?" shrieked Saffy. "That's my house! Why are they showing my house?"

"Well, Saffy and Harry, I have to tell you that there is a Vulpes Syndicate cell operating under right your whiskers! Have you seen many rattus rattus in your garden? We have reports from Bert the beefburger that there has been a sudden increase in rattus rattus in the fields. You will need to investigate this with the support of the other kitties here. If it is true that the Vulpes are operating under your whiskers, you will need all the help you can get!"

Harry gulped! His whiskers twitched and tail swished. He hadn't expected anything like this to happen to him. He had only come to stay with Saffy whilst his mummy was away. Now he was being made into an agent who would tackle international crime! He wasn't sure what to do at all. He stared at his special box and then looked at Saffy, who was also staring at her special box. "What's happening, Saffy?"

"Ooo, Harry, look. I have ordered us four boxes of Happeelix, and they will be delivered tomorrow! I have also ordered some bubbles and some ham and special treats!"

"Are you supposed to be doing that, Saffy? I thought the special boxes were just for spy business?"

Saffy purred with delight. "It will be fine Harrrrryyyy."

"OK, agents. We shall have a tuna and roast duck pancake lunch now. Then I will give you all the mission!"

With that, the mole jumped down from the platform and headed to the end of the long table. "Follow me," he cried, and each of the kitties jumped down and followed. To their delight, the ferrets had packed the table with not only tuna and roast duck pancakes but ham and cheese, fish fingers, and cream trifle.

"Is there any mousee?" asked Forest. He fancied a quick drink to boost his brave heart.

"Sorry, Forest. We don't drink at lunchtime. It spoils your brain for the afternoon, you know," pipped up the professor.

"*Harrumph!*" exclaimed Forest. He slunk off and looked in the little bag he brought with him and had hidden under the table. It had a little silver paw flask with some emergency mousee in it. He would have that later, he thought. He went back to the table and joined the others in tucking into the feast.

"I shouldn't eat the cream trifle. I am on a regime you know," proclaimed Edie. "I look this good because I take care of myself."

"Then I will eat yours, if you don't mind," responded Luna with a giggle and a roll of her golden eyes.

Mabel sniffed the air and twirled her whiskers. She wasn't impressed with what she had seen so far. She didn't like technology. She liked the honey-honey approach when she could schmooze her way to success. She did like tuna, though, and thought she would give that a try.

Harry and Saffy thought everything on the table looked good. Harry fetched Saffy some fish fingers and roast duck pancakes. He knew they were her favourite snax ever!

Fifi brought some cream trifle over to Harry and Saffy. "Would you like to have some of this trifle? The cream is really good," she said, licking her whiskers.

Harry took a quick glance at Saffy before he replied; he wasn't sure if Saffy would like him talking to Fifi. But Saffy looked happy enough as she sniffed the bowl. "Do you think it will go well with roast duck?" asked Saffy with a thoughtful look.

"I don't see why not," mused Fifi. Then they were all dipping the roast duck in the trifle and licking the cream off thoughtfully. "Mmm, I really like that, Saffy," said Fifi.

"Good choice," said Harry and grinned.

Louis and Luna were busy building fish finger towers and seeing if they could claw the fish fingers out one by one without the towers falling over. "Is that what they called fishanga?" Gina asked with a giggle. She had seen the hoomans play a game like that. Stella watched on, and then Harry noticed she had gone over to speak to Professor Mole. She was sharing the professor's worms! Harry couldn't believe it. They were deep in discussion, but Harry couldn't quite hear what they were talking about. But it looked serious.

"OK, my little agents, now you have had your lunch, I want to finish our training session. Then you can make your journeys home. I will tell you what you all need to do," Professor Mole announced.

All the kitties went back to their cushions on the chairs and sat bolt upright to listen to what he had to say. Everyone looked very serious, their eyes round in anticipation. Harry and Saffy noticed that Stella sat near the platform close to the professor.

"Now that you have learnt some pawcraft, I want you all to practice sending messages to each other. We are going start on the first take, which is to investigate what is happening on Saffy's farm. We have heard that the rattus rattus are working in the area, and that must mean that the Vulpe are operating close by. We need to find out what they are doing and report back to Stella, who will keep a record and send updates to me. Use your secret boxes wisely. We will need your first report tomorrow night."

"Crikey, Saffy, that doesn't give us long at all," whispered Harry.

"It's OK, Harry. Don't worry. We can do this," replied Saffy.

Before they all took their leave of spy school, Professor Mole taught them the spy school song, which went like this:

> We are friends; we are spies.
> Give the rattus a surprise.
> We are friends; we have fans,
> Finding out the rattus plans.
> We are cats; we are tigers,
> We fight the foxy as insiders!
> We are cats; we are agents,
> Rattus rattus, meet your assailants!
> We are friends; we are spies,
> Give the rattus a surprise.
> We are friends; we are spies,
> Give evil foxy a *big* surprise.
> We are agents, cats times ten,
> Get our paws in rattus dens.

We are agents, cats times ten,
Lead my moley to your den.
Rattus, rattus, be aware,
We have smoke bombees and secret hair!
Rattus rattus, run and hide!
Harry and Saffy side by side!

19

The Big Reveal

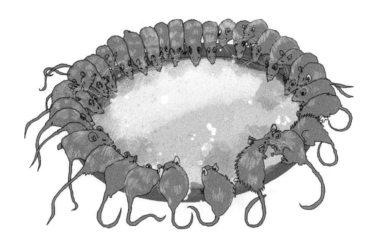

Professor Mole had told them all to take care on the way home. They mustn't lose their special boxes or the little bottle of ink and the smoke bombee. Each kitty was given a special bag made to be exact the colour of their fur. Forest decided to put his silver paw flask in the bag; there was just enough space. He was going to ditch the bottle of ink if he couldn't fit his silver paw flask in the bag, but everything fit together, so it worked out fine.

The kitties made their way to the Oxfordian Town rail station, there was quite a few of them, and they created quite a sight as they weaved their way through the hoomans and the busy streets. When they arrived at the station, Saffy asked Fifi which caterpillar she was going to catch. "One to Diddy Cottage. It doesn't take long at all. I will be back with my mummy very soon," Fifi replied with a twizzle of her whiskers."

"It takes us such a long time," said Saffy with a sigh.

She was just going to continue when Stella strolled up and whispered to her, "Mr Macgrumpy will pick you both up at the station, Saffy. I told him when you will be there."

"Oh, thank you, Stella. That is very kind of you. How do you know Mr Macgrumpy?"

"I have known him and Bert a long time, Saffy, I used to visit the farm before my family moved. Bert is lovely. He is one of us, you know. And you need to meet Culin the pig. He is also one of us. They will both help you with you pawmission." Stella had a big smile as she spoke.

"What? They are agents like us?" Saffy squealed.

"Shush, Saffy. People will hear you. We must be careful," said Harry as he glanced around him to check if anyone had been listening.

"Saffy, have you seen a dirty white and grey cat with hard black eyes around your garden?" asked Stella quietly.

Saffy gasped. "Do you mean Macavity? Yes, he is there all the time. and he comes into the house!"

"Beware of him, Saffy," continued Stella. He works with the rattus rattus, and we think he is connected to the Vulpe. He is very dangerous, and you need to watch him very carefully. You must use your special box to keep us informed as to his every movement."

"See, Saffy, I said he was a bad one!" Harry reminded her. "I was right. He *is* scary!"

"He is more than scary, Harry. He is *dangerous*," Stella advised.

"OK, I get the pawture of him. We will keep a close whisker on him!" replied Saffy as she rolled her golden eyes! "I am not frightened of him. I will sort him out!"

"Let's hope that is true, Saffy," remarked Stella. But she knew Saffy would be a force to be reckoned with. And Harry would always be there to help her.

Just at that moment Forest wobbled up to them. He had finished his mousee from his silver paw flask on the way to the station, and it had gone straight to his legs. The mousee had made them like jelly. "Saaaaffeeeee, can I come home with you, pleeeeeeeese." Forest hiccupped. His whiskers drooped, and his ears twitched. "We can partee Saaffffee."

Saffy looked at him in dismay. "Are you OK, Forest?? Your voice is very strange indeed! I am not sure my mummy would be very happy to see you like this!"

Harry looked on and remembered how he felt when the bubbles had gone to his paws. "Saffy," Harry whispered, "I think he should come with us. I am not sure how he will get home like this. I am sure your mummy will be OK. She is very kind, after all. We can help him, and he can help us find out what the rattus rattus are doing. What do you think?"

"OK, Harry, if you think that. But if he has furballs, then you will have to clean them up, you know," replied Saffy.

"OK, Forest, you can come with us. But you need to give me your silver paw flask so you don't have any more mousee!" announced Saffy.

Forest was thrilled. He giggled and burped. "That's smassshing, Saaafffeee. I haven't got any mousee left, I am afraid!"

Suddenly, the electric caterpillar appeared. "This is our caterpillar, Harry; let's go," Saffy ordered.

They both grabbed Forest, waved goodbye to Stella, and jumped on the caterpillar. It felt like a very, very long journey home for Harry as he spent most of his time trying to stop Forest from jumping up and down off the caterpillar seats and running up and down the caterpillar corridor! Saffy watched on, her golden eyes narrowed. She really hoped that the mousee's effects would stop before she had to introduce Forest to her mummy, or she was sure Mummy would think he was Freaky Forest!

They arrived at HiddeyHole and Tail Station just as it was going dark. "Come on, Saffy. We are home. Come on, Forest!" Forest was starting to feel a lot like himself and didn't need any help jumping from the caterpillar.

They were met by Mr Macgrumpy across the field. They climbed up into his tractor and sat on the hard red seats. "Have a good day?" mumbled Mr Macgrumpy. "Been busy at all?"

"Oh, yes," replied Saffy. "We have had a fantastic day, very exciting, we—" Harry poked her with his claw. Saffy jumped, and her golden eyes widened. "We went shopping for different types of Happeelix, you know. We had a lovely lunch with roast duck and cream trifle. Harry saw some lovely pictures in a shoppee, and we met our new friend, Forest."

"Mmmm. Sounds like a good day to me," replied Mr Macgrumpy. "I have just been going up and down the fields in my tractor. Then I noticed that some sheds had been emptied. I didn't know what for, and …" He drifted on to talk about the weather. Harry listened and wondered whether this was everyday farming stuff. He would ask Saffy later.

They arrived at the bottom of the road to the farm. "This is where you leave me," said Mr Macgrumpy. "Have a good evening and see you soon."

"Thank you, Mr Macgrumpy. It was very kind of you to meet us. We will see you soon." Saffy gave him a big purr; Harry and Forest followed suit.

Then they all jumped down and walked up the road to the farm. It was really dark, and Harry thought he heard scuttling and whispering in the hedges. "Did you hear that, Forest? Saffy?" asked Harry.

"Yes, Harry, I heard that. I smell *rats,* Harry!" replied Forest. His whiskers twitched, and his black nose pointed up to the sky, sniffing. Sure enough, they saw a long scaly tail disappearing into the hedges. There were definitely rats—rattus rattus there.

"Not now, boys. We can't find them now. We need to get home as Mummy will be worried that we are outside and its dark. And she hasn't seen us all day!"

So Harry and Forest followed Saffy back to the farm. The door was open, and they could hear Saffy's mummy calling their names. Harry thought she sounded very worried. They ran quickly to her, twirling their tails. "Here you are! You two, where have you been?" Then Saffy's mummy noticed Forest. "Have you brought me another friend, Saffy?" Mummy's voice softened, and she smiled when she saw Forest. "Oh my, you are lovely!" she said as Forest's head bumped her legs. "You better all come in for some food and Happeelix! You must have had a very big adventure today. I haven't seen you since this morning!" Harry and Saffy purred to each other, and Forest ran in ahead of them.

"Harry, we will need to go and put our bags in my secret place in case Mummy spots them," whispered Saffy. "I will tell Forest to follow us to the secret place. We must be quick whilst Mummy is making our fud!" So they nudged Forest to follow them, and they quickly dashed off to the human wash place and into the secret hidey-hole, where they put their bags carefully out of sight. They knew they had to check on the secret boxes for messages, but they would do that later.

"Now where have you all gone?" they heard Saffy's mummy cry. So they played horsey as fast as they could down the corridor and back into the kitchen, where their fud was waiting for them!

20

Discovering Traitors: Rats and Cats

Harry woke with a start. Sunshine was streaming through the window. *Goodness*, he thought, *what time is it? Am I late?* Saffy was nowhere to be seen, so he jumped down from the bedroom blanket tower and made his way down the corridor to the kitchen.

He could hear Saffy talking to Forest in the kitchen. She seemed to be explaining something to him, who was purring in agreement.

"Well, it's like this, Forest. Harry and I order as much Happelix as we want. We press these buttons on the box, and then a hooman delivers it all in the afternoon," she said proudly. Harry gasped. Saffy had gotten her special box from the secret place and was ordering Happeelix on it! Suddenly, the special box pinged loudly and turned bright red. The following message arrived:

> Agent Saffy, we have seen
> Something naughty on your box screen.
> We said they watch in every place, and now they know!
> *You are disgraced*!
> We see you ordered happy treats, no doubt
> For you and Harry to eat.
> You sent them to your mummy's farm, from
> A spy box, so she's at harm!
> Agent Saffy, may we remind

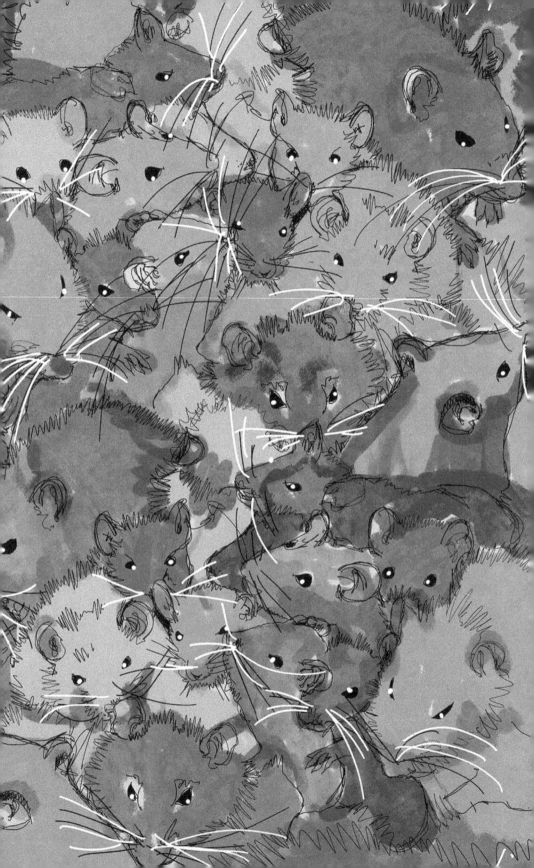

The rattus rattus ... are not kind!
They'll track your mummy down to you.
They will leave their spywear in her shoe!
The global HQ of Mr Sly the Fox
Is near your blanket tower box.
You must stay on red alert
To ensure that no one gets hurt.
Agent Saffy, please do learn,
For to be told off, it was your turn!
No more happy treats on your box.
We must defeat Mr Sly the Fox!

Saffy, Harry, and Forest gasped in unison! Saffy's golden eyes widened. "What have I done, Harry?" she cried. "Do you think the foxes will come for Mummy? How can we stop them?"

"I think it will be OK, Saffy. But we must never order Happeelix on the special box again. Purrromise me you won't," said Harry.

"I won't do it again, Harry. I purrromise," replied Saffy. Her tail had disappeared under her, and her ears were flat. And she had wet eyes!

"It's OK, Saffy. Don't worry. We will sort everything out! We won't let them get your mummy! Come on; let's make a plan for today after we've had our breakfast!"

Saffy cheered up at that idea. The three kitties horsied to the kitchen to see if their bowls were full. They were delighted to see that Saffy's mummy had filled their bowls and topped with Happeelix. They munched happily. As they finished, Saffy stretched and asked, "So Harry, what is our plan for today?"

"Well, Saffy," Forest jumped in, "I think we need to go and look for the rattus rattus. I smelt them last night, Saffy. I *smelt* them you know!"

"I agree, Forest," Harry commented. "We also need to speak to Bert and get him to introduce us to Culin the pig. And then we need to speak to Mr Macgrumpy to learn what has been happening with the buildings around the farm. Then we can make our report to Stella."

They dashed through the patio doors and up the three steps past the smelly bumblebee lavender place. And just as they were jumping over the lumps in the lawn, the dinosaurs came running out to meet them. "Saffy, Saffy, something dreadful has happened! Our eggies are missing!" Lady Ginge screeched! "Someone has taken them, and it was not Mummy! I know she comes and collects them and then makes gorgeous cakes with them. But she hasn't been, and the eggies are not there! We laid loads of eggies as well! Come and look in our house and see if you can find them!"

Harry stopped to ponder. His whiskers twitched in delight. Was he about to be Harry Bond and give those rats a fright? He needed to find the eggies and the thieves. He would bring those bad-uns to their knees!

The dinosaurs' house was too small for all three kitties to get inside, so Saffy and Harry went in to look around, while Forest stayed outside. After all, the KFCs couldn't let just *any* cat into their house; they had to know them! Inside, Harry thought it was very dark and quite smelly. He found some small squiggy eggs in the corner, and asked Lady Ginge what they were. "Oh, Harry Cat, they are just overcooked eggies, nothing like what we normally lay. Those aren't the ones we have lost," she replied.

In the meantime, Saffy was sniffing in the dinosaurs' bed. *This is an awful job,* she thought. *Why don't they use a kitty-litty tray which was cleaned?* Dirty dinos! Then she noticed that there were holes in the beds, and air was coming up from the ground. "Lady Ginge, what is this? Why do you have holes in your beds?" asked Saffy/

"We haven't, Saffy," screeched Lady Ginge.

"But you have. I can see them, and air is coming up from the ground. Didn't your bottoms get cold when you sit in beds?"

"That's very personal, Saffy," retorted Lady Ginge.

Whilst the two of them were arguing, Harry went to look more closely. Yes, the holes went into the ground from the dinos' house. "Forest," shouted Harry, "can you see any holes around the outside of the dinos' house?"

"Yes, and the holes smell of rattus rattus," replied Forest. Sure enough, when Harry went to look, there were holes all around the dinos' house. *These are tunnels,* he thought. *I wonder where they go?*

"Thank you, Lady Ginge", said Harry, "for letting us have a look inside your house. We think we know how your eggies are disappearing. They are falling into the ground underneath your house, and then I think they are being taken away. We will find out what is happening to them and let you know. In the meantime, try not to lay the eggies in the beds. Lay them in the corner of your house. They may be safe that way and not fall into the ground! Come on, Saffy and Forest. Let's see what we can find!"

Forest started sniffing around the dinos' house and the ground to pick up any rats' trails. He started out across the garden and ran to the edge, where the gullies could be found. Harry and Saffy followed him, wondering where this was going to lead them. Sure enough, when they got to the gullies, they could see the claw prints of the rats. "Let's see how far they go," said Forest, who horsied off down the gullies.

Harry shuddered. He hated rats and didn't want to meet them whisker to whisker. "Come on, Harry," Saffy said, having sensed his trepidation. "It will be OK. I know it will," she purred.

"But we haven't got our special bags with the smoke bombees and special Happeelix, Saffy. What will we do if we meet them whisker to whisker?" asked Harry.

"We are just going to investigate, nothing more. Then we will report to Stella."

They followed Forest, who was far ahead with his whiskers in the air. They continued far, far down the field, until they were nearly at the road where Mr Macgrumpy had picked them up to go to HiddeyHole and Tail Station. The gullies suddenly changed direction and ran behind small trees before stopping at a dark, dirty, stinky shed that looked like it hadn't been used in a while.

"Harry, I think we ought to ask Bert if he knows what's happening here," suggested Saffy in a low voice. "He might be able to tell us something."

"Yes, Saffy. And he could introduce us to Culin the pig as well," replied Harry.

At that moment, Forest came horseying back to them. "Hey, guess what! Guess what! I found the eggies! They're over here!"

They all horsied back to where Forest had been looking, but all they found was a large pile of empty eggshells! Saffy gasped. "What have they done to them? Where have they put the eggies?"

"Come on, Saffy, I think we should look in the stinky shed if we can," said Harry.

The Stinky Shed

They all crept up to the door of the stinky shed. It was slightly ajar as the wooden door had warped with age. Forest said, "Stand on my back, Saffy. Then you can see more through the gaps." Saffy jumped up on Forest's back. It was slippery, and she almost fell. But she dug her claws in, and poor Forest let out a long and loud *meow*. She looked through the gap. It was dark, but she could see something through the gloom. In the shadows was a *fox*! The Vulpes Syndicate was here! Saffy gasped and realised that she needed to keep very quiet. She looked further into the darkness and saw a network of tubes. There were also big, fat, gleaming pots and rows of bottles. The fox was studiously looking at the bottles.

"Saffy, I can smell mousee. I'm sure I can smell mousee," exclaimed Forest.

Saffy jumped down. "Come on, Harry. Come on, Forest. We need to get away from here as quickly as possible and make our report to Stella. I don't quite know what is going on there."

"But Saffy, we were going to find Bert and Culin. Aren't we going to do that now? I think we should, you know," replied Harry.

"Yes, I agree, Harry," said Forest. "Let's find them, Saffy. They can't be far away. We need to go through the gullies and out into the field. We are sure to see him there."

So off they went. They horsied off down the gullies, back through the trees, and out into the gullies at the edge of the field. They could see Bert in the distance. Harry wondered what they were going to say to Bert. Saffy would know what to say. But she hadn't said what she saw in the stinky shed. He wondered why because she was certainly keen to get away from there.

"Hello, Bert," called Saffy as they drew close to him. "How are you? Still dodging the freezer? We are here with our new friend, Forest. Say hi, Forest. Anyway", Saffy gabbled on quickly. "Bert, we need to understand what you know about the stinky shed."

"Saffy, Saffy, slow down, will you?" exclaimed Bert. "Hello, Forest. How are you? Are you enjoying your stay here?"

"Yes, thank you, Bert. But I keep smelling rats and mousee."

"What's mousee, Forest?" asked Bert.

"It's a drink that makes your paws dance, and you jump up and down. It looks like creamy custard, you know!"

Bert lowered his head and blew heavily out of his hairy nostrils. "Well, Saffy, strange things have been happening around here. There are lots and lots of rats moving around. They are stealing the eggies from the dinosaurs and taking them to the stinky shed. That shed has been empty for ages, and Mr Macgrumpy took all the rubbish out of it the other day. The next thing we see are the foxes moving lots of tubes and pans into the stinky shed. I have heard that it is the HiddeyHole and Tail Vulpe Syndicate, but we can't be sure."

"I saw a fox in the stinky shed today," admitted Saffy. "He was looking at bottles!"

"I knew it," exclaimed Forest. "They are making mousee!"

"Yes, I think you are right, Forest," Bert remarked. "We need to go into the stinky shed and see exactly what they are making. Then we need to destroy it and catch the members of the syndicate, if it is them who are doing this!"

"But why would they be making mousee?" asked Saffy.

"Well, it's very expensive, and everyone wants it for their parties," prompted Forest.

"You are quite right, Forest," replied Bert. "It is normal practice for the Vulpes Syndicate to make alcoholic drinks to sell, so they can then buy blood diamonds! Mousee can be made from eggies, and that could be a reason the dinos are having their eggs stolen."

"So what do we do next, Bert?" asked Saffy.

"Bert, will Culin the pig be able to help us? Stella told us he is one of us," Harry asked.

"Ah, Harry, that's a good question. Culin lives very close to the stinky shed. He may be able to tell us what he has seen and heard. Let's go and ask him," replied Bert.

The ground was very muddy, and Bert suggested the three kitties sit on his back, so they wouldn't get stuck in the mud. Bert took them into a clump of small trees. It was quite dark, but they could just make out a wooden house with cabbage leaves outside its door. "Culin, Culin, are you there?" called Bert, "It's Bert, and I have Harry, Saffy, and Forest with me. We need to have a quick word with you if that's OK."

There was a strange snuffling noise and some grunts as a large orange and black head poked itself out of the door. Two enormous nostrils breathed steam. The creature's eyes were covered by floppy, hairy ears. "Now what's all this? What's all this? I haven't eaten my cabbage yet!" came a deep voice. The beast tossed his head to reveal small, smiley, brown eyes. He pulled his big body out of the house and walked towards where Bert stood. Culin looked up at Bert and caught sight of the kitties on Bert's back. He smiled. "See you have some passengers there, Bert. What's this all about?"

"Well, Harry, Saffy, and Forest have been to Oxfordian Town, if you get my drift." Bert winked knowingly. "Stella has advised them to come and talk to you. I think they're interested in what has been happening in the stinky shed, you know."

"Umm, now let's see what I know," replied Culin. "A few days ago, Mr Macgrumpy was here with his tractor machine and took lots of rubbish away. Then the rattus rattus started coming around. They stole my cabbage, you know. I was really cross with them, cheeky blighters!"

"Crikey Culin, did you see them with any eggies?" asked Saffy. She felt quite shy around this orange and black hunk of a pig. "The dinosaurs have had their eggies stolen. Forest has smelt a rat or two, and then we saw lots of eggshells outside the stinky shed."

CULIN

"Well yes, little kitty, I have seen the rattus rattus carrying eggs into the shed in the night. The shells glow in the dark, you know. It's quite spooky to see," replied Culin. "But most important, I have seen four foxes sneaking around. And then a small van comes very early in the morning and takes red boxes away. They make a chinking noise, as if there is some glass or something in there."

"See, see. It's mousee," exclaimed Forest. "They are making mousee!"

"Now we don't know that for sure," replied Harry. "But we need to check it out!"

Saffy sat on Bert's back, which she thought was very comfy. She was more interested in the four foxes. Who were they? Culin's information confirmed what Bert told them. They just needed to find out about the foxes.

"Culin, have you seen the faces of the four foxes? Do you think you could recognise them if you saw them on an Identifox? We could ask Stella if she had some pictures of them," Saffy suggested in a ponderous way.

"I am sure I could, little kitty," mused Culin carefully.

"That's really helpful, Culin, Thank you," said Harry. "I think we should go and send our report to Stella. We'll ask her if she can send us any Identifox information."

"Good plan, Harry," Saffy commented, "Culin, have you got a special box that we could send you a message, or we could Pawtime you? Would that be OK?"

"Well, little kitty, it just happens that I have a special box, and you can send me messages if you type in the code: TNUGR RESHAR TNUGR. I will expect your message later tonight. I think we have to act quickly if it is the HiddeyHole and Tail Vulpe Syndicate."

"We better get back to the farm and send our report to Stella. We have a lot to do," said Saffy. And with that they said goodbye to Culin, and they hoped he enjoyed his cabbage.

Bert started back slowly to the farm. When they arrived at the hedge, they thanked Bert for his help. "Can we get you anything Bert?" Saffy asked.

"Well, I would appreciate a nice bit of cow cake," Bert said, smiling. "I haven't had any for ages."

"We will have some delivered to you, Bert. I can order it from the box. It will be with you super quick," replied Saffy.

The three kitties horsied back through the garden and into the house. Saffy checked to see where her mummy was. She was busy on the box, tip-tapping way for her work. Saffy wasn't sure what her work was, but it paid for the Happeelix, and that's what counted. Saffy meowed to Harry and Forest to creep past her mummy and to go to the special hidey-hole in the human washing place. There they would be able to send their report to Stella.

Saffy took her special box out of her bag. "Shall I send the report to Stella?" she asked.

"We could write to her in invisible ink and use your loo roll, Saffy," suggested Forest.

"I think that would take quite a long time. And it would be a very big bird once we made it," Harry pointed out. "I think it's best if Saffy sends the report from the special box."

Saffy pawed at the special box, and it started to glow. Could she remember how to send a message to Stella? She frowned at the screen. She extended her claw and clawed down the list of kitty names until she found Stella. Now what should she say. They had found out so much! She started pawtyping:

> alletS,
> eW evah dnouf eht yknits dehs!
> Siege evha neeb nelots
> treB si gnipleh su

What was happening? The special box was putting her message into kitty code! Saffy didn't know quite what to do, so she continue pawtyping:

> eW kniht eht sexof era ereh
> esaelp dnes su sotohp fo eht sexof, niluC lliw pleh su.
> lleT su tahw ot od txen
> evol H, S &F

111

Saffy stared at the screen. Would Stella understand it? She was a very clever cat. Saffy suddenly remembered that at St Gertrude's, Professor Mole said they would learn more pawcraft. Was this part of it? She showed the screen to Harry and Forest. Forest thought it was hilarious and wriggled on the floor in delight. "Saffy, that is wonderful, and I haven't even had any mousee today!" Forest cried with delight.

Harry frowned. He didn't understand this at all. "What does it say, Saffy?" he quizzed.

"Well, Harry, I said that we have found the stinky shed, that the eggies have been stolen, and that we think the foxes are there! I have also said that Culin will help us and asked what we should do next!"

"That's great Saffy," said Forest. "Well done! Are you going to send it now?" asked Forest. Saffy pressed her claw on the screen, and the message disappeared.

"It's gone, boys. I think it is going to Stella now." At that moment, they heard Saffy's mummy calling them for their dinner. "Stay here, Forest!" commanded Saffy. "You need to see if we get a message from Stella and check what she wants us to do. We will go and eat our fud. And when we have finished, we'll come back, and you can go and eat your dinner. Is that OK?"

Without waiting for his reply, Saffy told Harry to come along, and they disappeared off down the corridor to the kitchen, leaving poor Forest staring at the special box.

21

Catching the Guilty Ones

Harry and Saffy returned to the special hidey-hole to find Forest still staring at the special box. The special box was now flashing and beeping. "We must have a message from Stella," said Saffy. "Let's see what is says!"

"Saffy, is there any fud left in the kitchen for me," asked Forest sheepishly. "I am quite hungry now, and I don't want to be rude, but ..."

"Of course, Forest. I am so sorry. We should have brought some back with us, but we were so excited we forgot." admitted Saffy, "There is lots of fud and snax in the kitchen. You go and help yourself. We will check the message. And when you have finished, you can come back and see what we need to do next."

With that, Forest headed off to the kitchen. They could hear Saffy's mummy saying, "Awwww, Forest, you are such a polite boy. Fancy waiting until Harry and Saffy had eaten and then come to find food. I will give you some special tuna for that. I bet you love tuna." *Lucky blighter,* thought Harry. *I wish we had tuna!*

"Harry, look. Here is the message from Stella!" They both looked at the tiny screen. This time it wasn't in code, so they could read it straightaway!

> You little kitties have done so well.
> Forest can tell a problem from its smell!
> Confirmation that the rattus rattus are here gives us all mighty cheer.

You need to smash the mighty Vulpe quick,
Before they make more kitties sick.
Here is what you need to do:
Wait in the night to give the rattus rattus a fright.
They will run, and the foxes will too!
Use your smoke bombs in the stinky shed.
Smash the bottles so the Vulpe see red!
Gina will come along with others.
They will give the Vulpes lots of troubles.
Mr Macgrumpy, Culin, and Bert
Will fill the stinky shed with lots of dirt.
The Vulpes will lose all that they have;
Their strength in HiddeyHole and Tail will cave.
You will beat them all tonight if you get your timing right!

"Well, there you go, Harry. That's what we need to do," Saffy said excitedly.

"But we haven't got any pictures of the foxes to show Culin," pointed out Harry.

"Wait, Harry, there is another message here!" Sure enough, when they clicked on the message, photos of four very frightening foxes popped up. The first one had spikey silver fur and a sneering lip. He looked quite old and had the title Mr Vernon Fox:

Mr Vernon Fox

"Extremely Dangerous. Do Not Approach." The second one was a girl fox called Rubeeee Roxy Foxy.

She had bright red fur, bright red lipstick, and mean cold eyes. The third fox looked quite young, Harry thought. He was called Callum Cocky Fox.

Callum
Cocky Fox

Rubeee Roxy Foxy ♡

Next to his name it also said, "Extremely Dangerous. Do Not Approach." The last photo was of a mangy-looking fox. He had a dirty dripping snout and wild eyes. His title was Gunky Fox

He looks as mad as a box of frogs, thought Harry. Beneath each photo was the title "Member of the HiddeyHole and Tail Syndicate."

"Saffy, shall we send them to Culin to see if these are the same foxes he saw?" asked Harry. But before he had finished his question, Saffy had pressed the button, and the message was forwarded on to Culin. Harry and Saffy stared at the special box, waiting to see what Culin would say. Were these the same foxes he had seen, or were there even more foxes in the HiddeyHole and Tail Vulpe Syndicate that the NCA didn't know about?

Forest horsied back into the hidey-hole and nearly fell into the two of them as they stared into the special box. "Have you been on the mousee again, Forest?" Saffy asked haughtily.

"I wish I had, Saffy," Forest replied with a grin. "I wish I had, but I think I will have to wait for my mousee until I get home to Lewesland."

The special box buzzed and glowed green. Saffy pressed the screen, but nothing happened! *What? What is happening?* she wondered.

"I think you need to purr into the screen," whispered Forest.

So she did: *Purrrrr, purrrrr.*

Suddenly, Culin's snout app
Harry. *I don't like looking up his s*

Mr. Gunky Fox

"Little kitties, little kitties, I have seen the photos! Yes, these foxes are exactly who I have seen! So what's the plan, kitties? What are we going to do?" Culin snorted.

"Culin, Stella has sent us a plan, but I think we need to work out who will do what. Shall I read it to you?" asked Saffy.

"Gone on then, little kitty. Let's hear it!"

So Saffy read Stella's message. Forest listened carefully as he hadn't heard it yet. After she finished Stella's instructions, Culin snorted deeply. "Well, I can certainly help you smash the bottles if we can get into the stinky shed. I can ask Bert to contact Mr Macgrumpy. He can bring his tractor to move the dirt into the shed."

Harry thought that this was a great idea! He was thinking how he could give the rattus rattus a fright. Then the idea came to him! "Hey everyone, I have had an idea about freaking out the rattus rattus. What if we waited for them to bring the eggies to the stinky shed. And once they had the eggies in the shed, we bring them some fud which has our special Happeelix in it. They will go to sleep, and then we can get Gina to come and collect them with a catching ring and hand them over to the NCA!"

"Harry, that's a great idea," Saffy said gleefully. "And I was thinking we can throw our smoke bombees into the shed to confuse the foxes, and then Mr Macgrumpy can come and put the dirt in the stinky sheds to stop them from escaping!"

"That's good, really good, kitties" slobbered Culin. He had just found some leftover cabbage and was hoovering it up with his snout. "But when am I going to smash the bottles?"

"What if after we throw the smoke bombee into the stinky shed, we race in and snatch as many bottles of mousee as we can? Then Culin can run in and smash the bottles. And when we run out, Mr Macgrumpy shoves the dirt in so they can't get out," suggested Forest.

"Mmmm, this all sounds very exciting." Saffy purred. "Culin, could you please ring Bert and ask him to ask Mr Macgrumpy to meet us at midnight near the stinky shed. He needs to know that we need his tractor to move the dirt. I will ring Gina and ask her advice on how to catch the rats all in one go!" Saffy was looking very pleased with herself. She really was turning into an agent. And she liked it!

"Saffy, I think we should make sure our special boxes are fully charged with lickelectricity. We may need to talk to Bert, Culin, and Stella during the night, and we need to make sure we have all the right pawcraft equipment in our bags," advised Harry.

"We will, Harry. Let's do that now. I am also going to take my purple ribbon! You never know when I might need it," remarked Saffy, her golden eyes wide like the moon! "Culin, could you also please ask Bert if he would pick us up by the hedge after the dinosaurs' house at nine o'clock? We don't want to get stuck in the mud. Then we can meet you near the stinky shed behind the little trees."

With that, Culin closed the call, and Harry was relieved not to have to see that snout so up close! He could see the bristles and steam, and it wasn't a pretty sight!

The three kitties made sure that their special boxes were fully charged. Then checked their bags for smoke bombees and the special Happeelix. Harry went into the kitchen to see what fud he could find to give to the rats. He found some chew sticks and biscuits, and he put them into his bag.

Saffy was on the special box to Stella. She had called her to update her on their plans. "Well done, Saffy, and good luck. I will call Gina and tell her to bring the rattus catching ring to help you trap them safely. We don't want them biting any of you!"

Saffy decided it would be a good idea for them all to go and sit with her mummy for a little while, until it was time for Bert to pick them up. Saffy's mummy was delighted to have all three kitties curl up with her on the soft pink sofa. She switched on the picture box and started to watch a movie, giving them treats as they all sat there together. Saffy's mummy started to close her eyes and was soon fast asleep.

"Good. Come on, Harry and Forest. Let's paddy-paws out of here whilst she won't miss us." It was nearly nine o'clock when the three kitties went through the lounge doors and up the lavender path to find Bert. The dinosaurs were all asleep in their little house. and Harry noticed some scaley tails of the rats sneaking off with the dinosaurs' eggies.

"Come on, Saffy and Forest. We will need to meet Bert and go to the stinky shed as quickly as we can to catch the rats with the eggies," exclaimed Harry.

They saw Bert on the horizon. Harry stopped to ponder, and his whiskers twitched with delight. Was he about to be Harry Bond and give the rats a fright? He could do the smoke bombee, or he could do a disguise. The rattus rattus would never know Harry's big surprise.

Harry and Saffy rode on Bert's back, but Forest decided to walk behind them, treading carefully through the mud that had gone hard in the night's frost. He wanted to see if anyone was walking behind them and to keep his whiskers sharp for any new smells!

When they approached the stinky shed, they could see the rattus rattus taking the eggies into the shed one by one. The eggies glowed white in the moonlight. They looked like a string of big pearls on the move!

"Saffy, I'll put the special Happeelix on the snax I have and then go and tempt the rattus rattus with them," said Harry.

Saffy's whiskers twitched with excitement. "Good plan, Harry, and good luck. When they are eating, you and I can through the smoke bombees into the stinky shed and confuse the foxes! I hope Culin is ready to smash the bottles. Then Mr Macgrumpy can push all the dirt into the stinky shed to stop the foxes from escaping!"

Harry jumped down from Bert's back. The ground was cold and hard, and it made his paws sting. But he was almost too excited to notice as he got the snax ready for the rattus rattus. He crept forward, keeping low to the ground, until he was very close to the rats and the eggies. "What's that? Who is it?" one of the rats squeaked.

"Hello, my friends. How are you all on this cold night?" purred Harry. His purr was calm, but he had bees buzzing in his tummy fur again! *Keep calm,* he thought. He strolled onward. "I thought you deserved some yummy treats after all your hard work tonight!"

"We don't know you," snapped the largest rat. He had big fangs that glowed in the dark and huge claws! He was quite a terrifying sight.

"Well, Mr Vernon Fox sent me to find you and give you these," replied Harry, dropping the snax in front of the rats.

They all looked at the tempting pile of goodies and licked their fangs in delight. They didn't take much persuading as they all jumped into the pile and started to stuff their cheeks, munching away in the moonlight. One by one the rats started to yawn and lick their whiskers. One of them stretched and then curled up asleep. The others soon followed suit, and Harry was surrounded by a circle of sleeping rats!

He jumped over them and ran back to Saffy. Forest was nowhere to be seen. "I did it, Saffy. The special Happeelix worked, and they are all asleep! Where is Forest? What has happened to him?" Harry was worried about Forest.

"Don't worry, Harry. Forest has gone to get Culin and Mr Macgrumpy. They will be here soon," replied Saffy. Just as she finished explaining, Forest and Culin appeared through the trees. Behind them, two yellow eyes crept forward. It was Mr Macgrumpy in the tractor! The tractor stopped a few pawprints away from them, and the eyes closed.

"Hello, little kitties. Everything OK?" Culin snorted.

"Shh, Culin. We have to be really velvet-pawed here to surprise the foxes," scolded Saffy. Culin shook his big ears and grinned. This was going to be exciting! "Do you know the plan, Culin?" she asked. "We are going to throw the smoke bombees into the stinky shed. Then you can go in and smash the bottles whilst the foxes are confused. Mr Macgrumpy will then come and push the dirt into the shed to stop them from escaping!"

"Good plan, Saffy. Yes, that's all good with me," agreed Culin.

With that Harry, Saffy, Forest, and Culin approached the stinky shed. The rickety door was slightly ajar. They could see the four foxes cracking the eggies and then putting the yolks into a huge vat. The vat made a huge clanking noise, and the foxes had to shout at each other to make themselves heard. "How many bottles of mousee are we going to make tonight, Vernie?" Rubeeee Roxy Foxy asked, her lips shining bright red.

"That depends on whether those pesky rats have given us enough eggies for the job," replied Vernon.

"Well, we have lots and lots of bottles ready here from last night" gloated Gunky, spitting as he spoke. "We will have loads of mousee to sell. One-Eye Sly Fernandez will be *so* pleased with us!"

"Harry, Forest, we need to throw the smoke bombees really quickly, before the rats wake up. Gina still has to bring her catching ring, don't forget," proclaimed Saffy as she edged closer to the door. Forest and Harry followed her, ready with their smoke bombees. The rickety door creaked as Saffy pushed it open. But fortunately, the noise of the vats covered the sound. "On the count of three paws, throw the bombees, boys," whispered Saffy, "One paw, two paws, three paws. Go!" With all their might, they threw the smoke bombees into the stinky shed.

They waited with saucer eyes, not quite sure what was going to happen next. Nothing! Nothing happened. They looked at each other in dismay. What were they going to do now? Forest started sniffing. He drew his eyes closed and sniffed again. "Something is going to happen in a minute, guys," he whispered.

"How do you know?" asked Harry.

"I can smell it, remember?" Sure enough, one of the little smoke bombs started to puff smoke. Then the other two started to do the same.

Callum Cocky Fox looked up from where he was counting bottles. "Hey guys, can you smell that?" he asked.

"Probably Gunky dropping a trump," sneered Ruby.

"I beg your pardon," snapped Gunky. "It's not me today!"

Suddenly, the smoke bomb burst open, and the whole shed was engulfed in thick white smoke. The foxes started barking and screaming.

Culin barged into the stinky shed, smashing bottles with his big hooves and bashing his bottom against the shelves so that the bottles fell to the ground and cracked. The smoke was getting really think now. "Come out. Come out, Culin," Saffy yelled. "Don't get stuck in there!"

"I can't see you, Saffy. Where are you?" shouted Culin.

"We'll rub our furry sides on the door. Then you can smell how to get out," called Forest (He did know all about smells, after all!) The three kitties rubbed themselves against the door as quickly as they could! "Can you smell that, Culin?" Forest asked.

"Yessss," Culin replied with a grunt. And he charged out of the stinky shed.

The foxes were running around trying to find a way out. They crashed into the tubes and cut their paws on the smashed glass. They screamed— and cursed!

"Where is Mr Macgrumpy," asked Saffy. We need to get the door blocked now!

Boooooom, booooom.

The stinky shed exploded!

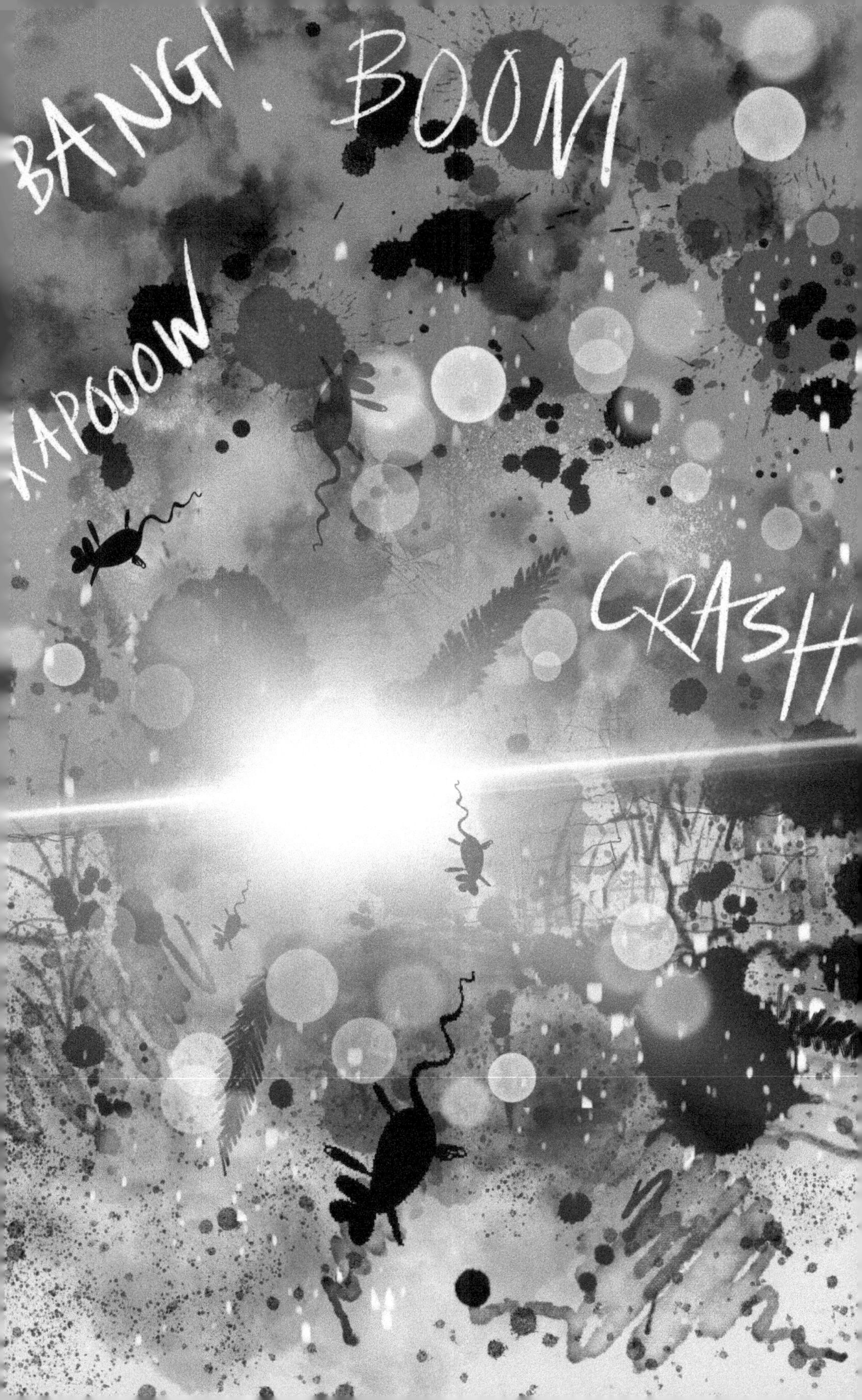
BANG!
BOOM
KAPOOOW
CRASH

The kitties and Culin ran as bits of stinky shed fell from the sky. Harry wasn't sure he didn't see a foxy tail floating away. Suddenly, the two yellow eyes appeared as Mr Macgrumpy drove the tractor towards the stinky shed. He pushed all the pieces of the shed together into a huge pile!

Through the smoke and the bits of flying shed, they saw a dark mound. A kitty stood on top, its tail standing tall. As they got closer, they could see it was Gina, wearing her big Cheshire Cat grin. She was standing atop of a mound of sleeping rats. And just for good luck, she kept digging her claws into the rats and biting the scaley tails that stuck out!

"Hi, guys! That's quite a show you put on!" Gina laughed a big laugh and purred with delight. "I got all these rattus rattus in the catching ring all safe and sound. Mr Macgrumpy can put them in a safe place until the NCA takes them away!"

"That's awesome," shouted Harry. He still had the *boooooom* from the shed ringing in his ears.

"Culin, are you OK?" asked Saffy. She looked a bit dishevelled, with her fur sticking up in places.

"Yes. I have had great fun!" Culin answered with gleam in his dark eyes, and a grunt. "But where is Forest? Has anyone seen Forest?"

Harry and Saffy peered through the darkness and smoke. Where was he? They were sure he had come out of the shed with them. Hadn't he?

Mr Macgrumpy and his tractor were busy shovelling the stinky shed into a large pile. He seemed to be really enjoying himself, humming away. "Mr Macgrumpy, have you seen Forest?" called Saffy.

"Nope!" was the brief reply.

He has to be here somewhere, thought Harry. "Maybe he is hiding somewhere," suggested Harry. He would turn up, he was sure.

"So what do we do now, Saffy?" asked Harry.

"I think we should call Stella and let her know what happened. She will tell us what to do next." She pulled her special box out of her bag and clawed in Stella's number. The special box went *buzzzz,* and Stella appeared on the screen. "Look, Stella," said Saffy as she showed Stella the pile of shed that Mr Macgrumpy had pulled together and Gina standing on the mound of rats! "Mission accomplished! I don't think the foxes are still around, and we caught all the rats! What shall we do now?"

"Well, Saffy, you need to check to see if any of the foxes are left. But I don't think they could survive those smoke bombs! Congratulations. You have all done really well on your first mission. Mr Macgrumpy will take the rats away and dispose of them. Don't worry about them; we will sort them out! We will see you at spy school very soon. Watch out for a message from the professor!"

Stella closed the call, and Saffy stared at the special box. Was that it? Nothing more to be done?

Harry and Culin looked at her little dismayed face. "Don't worry, Saffy," Harry assured her. "We did really well, and we didn't get hurt! Look, why don't you wear your purple ribbon on the way home. That will cheer you up, won't it?"

"Oh yes, Harry, it will! But first, let's check the shed pile for foxes. And we have to find Forest!"

The little gang went their separate ways. Culin, Bert, and Harry went over to the pile of shed. Saffy went off to look for Forest, and Gina went with Mr Macgrumpy to get rid of the rattus rattus. "See you later, guys," Gina called as she jumped up into the tractor cabin and headed off into the darkness.

The pile of shed was quite gruesome. Harry and Culin saw bits of fox fur sticking out, and Bert found a fox's tail. They weren't really sure if any of the foxes had escaped, but it certainly didn't look like it!

Culin decided he had enough excitement for one night. He wished Harry and Bert good night. "Thank you for all your help, Culin," said Harry. "See you tomorrow maybe."

"I am sure you will, little kitty," replied Culin as he headed off back to his house and his cabbage.

Harry jumped up on Bert's back and headed off towards the farm. They could just see Saffy in the distance. Harry called to her, "Any sign of Forest, Saffy?"

"No, not yet, Harry. I am still looking. I keep waving my purple ribbon to help him see me, but I am not sure it's working.

The three carried on towards the farm. When they got to the hedge, Harry jumped down from Bert's back. "Thanks, Bert, for all your help tonight. If you see Forest, can you let us know please?"

"Of course I will, Harry. I'm sure he will be OK."

Saffy ran on towards the farm. Just before the lavender steps, she saw something. A tail was sticking out from the lavender bushes—along with an empty bottle of mousee! There was Forest, giggling away. He saw Saffy and gave her a really big smile. "Harry, Harry, I have found him!" Saffy yelled.

Harry ran over to see what was happening. Forest looked at them both and let out a big, happy yowl. "Well, I couldn't let all the mousee go to ruin, could I? I took a couple bottles for us to celebrate with. I tell you what, it's good stuff!"

"Forest, what are you like?" squealed Saffy. "Good grief, what a night!"

"Tell you what, Saffy, I like that purple ribbon of yours," remarked Forest, a glint in his eye.

"Mmm. I think it's time we went to the blanket tower, Harry." Saffy smiled. "You can have the special fluffy cushion tonight. And Forest, and save some of that mousee for later!"

22

The Spy School Calls

Harry woke up to the sunlight streaming through the curtains onto the blanket banqueting tower. *Crikey* he thought. *What time is it?* Had they missed breakfast? He felt a gurgling in his fur tummy, and it growled loudly. He looked around to see if anyone had heard it.

Saffy was in a very deep sleep, with her purple ribbon still around her. She looked adorable, even though her fur was rather ruffled. Saffy's eyes popped wide open, like golden saucers. They glowed. "Is everything OK, Harry? Was last night real, or did I dream it?" Then she realised she still had her purple ribbon on. "Crikey, Harry it was *real,* wasn't it? We did catch the rattus rattus, and the smoke bombees blew up the stinky shed, didn't they?"

"We did, Saffy. It was so exciting. But I am so hungry now I could eat a whole tuna fish by myself. Shall we go and find some breakfast?"

"Good idea, Harry. And let's see if Forest is OK. I bet his head hurts from all the mousee he guzzled." She smiled and gave a *purrrrrr.*

They jumped down from the blanket tower and padded slowly down the corridor to the kitchen. They didn't feel like horsing around today after their big adventure. When they arrived in the kitchen, Forest was sitting by the glass doors, looking out into the garden. The dinosaurs had found his empty bottle of mousee and were pecking it and kicking it around the lawn. Lady Grey was leading the kick, and the other girls were trying to keep up with her, their feathers all a flutter.

"I see the dinosaurs like the mousee as well as I do," Forest said with a grin. "It gives you an appetite, you know. I have had two bowls of tuna and three Happeelix to go with it," he boasted.

"Is there anything left for us?" asked Harry.

Just then, Saffy's mummy returned to the kitchen. "Hello, you two. Would you like some breakie? Forest was so hungry this morning that he ate *all* the tuna, I'm afraid. But I have some sardines if you would like those." Harry and Saffy circled her legs, twisting their tails in delight at the sound of sardines. "Saffy, what have you done to you coat?" Saffy's mummy asked. "You will need a bath." Saffy pretended not to hear, sticking her head into the dish of sardines.

Harry had licked his bowl clean. He gazed up at Saffy's mummy and blinked his big green eyes in adoration. "Would you like some more, Harry? You are all so hungry this morning. I don't know what has been going on in the night." The three kitties glanced at each other and kept their heads low. "Have the rats been around again? Don't say the foxes turned up too?" Saffy's mummy commented. What did she know about the rattus rattus and the Vulpes Syndicate? Was she a spy too? Harry decided it was just a lucky guess. And with all the things Saffy's mummy did, she didn't have time to be a spy.

The three kitties took themselves off and lay stretched out on the soft pink sofa. "What shall we do now?" asked Forest. "I think I should head off home soon. My mummy and daddy will be worried about me, I am sure. Maybe they have made some of those paper thingies that you see in the street saying, "Lost Kitty", and with the most embarrassing description and photo of you that you could imagine. I would *hate* that!"

"I think we should check the special boxes to see if we have any messages from Stella or Professor Mole," replied Saffy. So they headed off to the human washing place and the hidey-hole. "Ah, ah", they heard Saffy's mummy call after them. "You need a wash, young lady!" *Not on your nelly,* thought Saffy as she disappeared into the hidey-hole.

Once inside, they all checked their special boxes. Saffy noticed that Forest had secured his bottle of mousee in the hidey-hole, along with her loo roll and candle. All the special boxes were glowing.

"Come on, Saffy, let's see what the messages are," said Harry excitedly. They all clawed the special boxes, and each one had the same message:

> Congratulations on succeeding in you mission.
> Return to spy school at 2 p.m. today.
> Bert will meet you to ride with Mr Macgrumpy to the HiddeyHole and Tail Station to catch the caterpillar.

"We better move quickly, Saffy, if we are going to get there for 2 p.m.," remarked Forest. So they put their special boxes in their bags.

Saffy noticed that Forest also secreted the mousee in his bag. "I shall wear my purple ribbon. I think it's a purple ribbon day."

They sneaked out of the hidey-hole and peeped down the corridor to see if Saffy's mummy was about. She was busy on the box, so they crept passed her and out the glass doors into the garden. Then up the lavender steps and past the dinosaurs' house, where the dinosaurs were still kicking the empty bottle of mousee. *They really are birdbrains,* thought Harry.

Bert was waiting for them at the hedge. "Everyone recovered from last night?" he asked. "What a night we had, didn't we? I could do it all again!"

"Mmm, not sure we could do it all again tonight," replied Saffy. "I really am quite tired today!"

"Oh, you will soon be OK. Jump up, and let's go and find Mr Macgrumpy," said Bert.

They rode on Bert until they got to where the stinky shed had been. All the rubbish from the explosion had been cleared away, and not a rattus rattus was to be seen! "Pity about the mousee getting smashed," said Forest ruefully. "It was really good stuff, you know!" Saffy gave him a sideways glance but decided it wasn't any good saying anything to Forest about mousee!

"Where has everything gone, Bert?" asked Harry.

"The NCA did a clean-up late last night, Harry. They checked everything out, and I think they made their own report. See what Professor Mole says today when you see him."

They could see Mr Macgrumpy on his tractor in the distance, ready to take them the caterpillar station. They jumped down from Bert's back. "Thank you, Bert. We will see you later," said Saffy as they went off to meet Mr Macgrumpy.

"Hello, Mr Macgrumpy. Everything OK with you?" asked Saffy. Mr Macgrumpy just nodded, grunted, and signalled them to get into the tractor.

Off they rocked to the caterpillar station, bumping along. Harry thought, *This doesn't get any better, no matter how many times you do it!* They arrived just in time as the caterpillar crawled into the station. "Jump on, everyone," shouted Saffy as the doors of the caterpillar opened. The three kitties jumped through hooman legs as they entered the caterpillar and hid under the seats.

"No running and jumping around this time, Forest," warned Harry.

"What? Did I do that last time?" Forest replied, coyly and grinned.

The caterpillar rumbled along, and Saffy listened to the announcements. "Our stop is next, boys. Get ready to go. And don't forget your bags!" The caterpillar crept into Oxfordian Town station.

"Do you remember how to get to St Gertrude's, Saffy?" asked Harry.

"Oh yes. And I have the special box to put us right in case we go the wrong way," Saffy said smugly. Off they went, retracing their paws past the Hanny pictures and the Catelonian Library until they reached the doors of St Gertrude's.

"Saffy, did you remember the wigglers?" Harry asked casually.

"Oh, crikey cod sticks. I forgot them! What will we do?"

"Maybe if we wait, someone will come out, and then we can dash in?" suggested Forest.

"Good plan, Forest," said Harry. So they sat and waited and waited and waited. It was getting quite late, well past two o'clock. The three kitties didn't know what to do. Should they call Stella on their special boxes? Harry wished he had that thought of that earlier. What would Professor Mole say? Hoomans walked passed them and cooed at how lovely they all looked, sitting there in a row!

"Maybe someone will come and look for us," whispered Saffy.

Just then, the little door creaked open, and Louis, the silver cat, poked his nose and whiskers outside. He spotted them sitting there and meowed for them to come in. "Where have you been?" he asked. "We have been waiting for you!"

"Well, we forgot the wigglers," admitted Saffy. "Never mind that. We must get to Professor Mole as quickly as we can!" They hurried across the courtyard and up the windy steps. Harry felt quite dizzy dashing up the steps! They arrived at the door to the dining room and stopped.

"Let's get our breath back before we go in," advised Louis. The kitties sat for a moment and licked their whiskers and paws.

"I am ready now," proclaimed Saffy as she drew herself up to her full height. Louis pushed the door open, and Harry, Saffy, and Forest had the biggest surprise ever!

The dining room was decorated with ribbons and paper streamers. The weasels were playing a strange untuneful song on some guitars made of wood and rubber bands. But it didn't matter. It was party time!

"Welcome agents! Well done on defeating the HiddeyHole and Tail Vulpes Syndicate," shouted Professor Mole above the noise. "We have a special celebration for you to honour you on the success of your first mission!"

Harry, Saffy, and Forest stood there with their tails held high! How wonderful to see all the other agents celebrating in their success. *I bet Mummy would love this,* thought Saffy. *She loves a good party!*

The dining table was full of fabulous fud—huge tuna steaks, fishy fingers, ham, and cheese. Happeelix abounded, and there was, of course, creamy trifle!

"Before we feast, I want us all to gather together around my platform. All come up to me, please," Professor Mole announced. All the kitties ran up to the platform, waiting to see what the professor would do next.

"Mabel, can you bring the golden stars to me please?" requested Professor Mole. Up strolled Mabel. Three golden stars on bright blue ribbons hung from her mouth. She looked very haughty and rather peeved, as if she wanted to keep them all to herself!

"Harry, Saffy, and Forest, please jump up on the platform," Professor Mole ordered. The kitties looked at each other and made a massive jump onto the platform. Harry almost skidded off the back of the platform as he mistimed his jump!

"Steady, steady, Harry. Come to me" requested Professor Mole. The three sat before the mole as he said, "In honour of your great success and bravery of eliminating the HiddeyHole and Tail Vulpe Syndicate, the NCA is awarding you the Star of Bravery!" And with that, the mole took the blue ribbons from Mabel and hung them around each little kitty's neck. All the agents gave a huge chorus of *meow.*

"Now everyone can feast," announced the Professor. All the kitties ran to the table and jumped up to enjoy all the treats.

Harry noticed that Forest was lapping up some mousee that he had snaffled into his silver paw flask. Harry smiled. *Oh, well. As long as he is enjoying himself and can make it back to the caterpillar station, so what?*

As Harry feasted on some tuna, Professor Mole wobbled up to him. "Harry, we have a special treat for you, Saffy, and Forest. We have a jelliwobbler in the courtyard that will take you all home in style!" *Crikey*, thought Harry. He had never been in a jelliwobbler before! He wondered what it would be like.

After all the treats had been snaffled, the professor indicated that they should follow him down to the courtyard, where the jelliwobbler was waiting. They said their farewells and promised to message each other on their special boxes.

The jelliwobbler sat on the grass with its wings waving around and around. "Get in everyone. Edie will take you home. See you all again soon," called the professor. The kitties jumped into the jelliwobbler, amazed that Edie could drive one of these things!

They sat there quietly as Edie pushed the buttons, and the jelliwobbler started to raise into the air! *Wooooooooooo!* The noise of the wings was extremely loud as they flew over Oxfordian Town, following the line of the river and across the fields. Saffy could see the farm below her. "Are we landing here, Edie?" She pointed to the farm with her claw.

Edie nodded, and then the jelliwobbler started to go down, down, down—until it landed in Marge's garden! "Right. Saffy and Harry, you can jump out here, and I will take Forest back to Lewesland!"

Harry really didn't want to jump into Marge's garden, but he thought he would be safe with Saffy by his side. So they both jumped out of the jelliwobbler, as agents do, and landed on the soft lawn. "Quick, Harry, run!" instructed Saffy. They bolted through Marge's hedges and back into their own garden.

"Phew! We made it, Saffy," said a very relieved Harry as they slowed down to pass the dinosaurs' house and down the lavender steps, past the bumblebees, and into the house through the glass doors.

"Hello, kitties. Have you had a nice time in the garden? Been playing amongst the flowers?" asked Saffy's mummy. "Come on. I will give you some snacks and treats if you like!"

Saffy and Harry smiled at each other. If only Saffy's mummy knew what had gone down today, she wouldn't believe them!

23

Going Home

The next couple days were idyllic for Harry. He and Saffy lazed about the house and played Fish Fish on the box. It was a new game that Harry hadn't seen before. But Saffy knew all about it and was very good at chasing and catching the little colourful fishes that dashed across the screen. They enjoyed the warm sun in the garden. They wandered amongst the lavender but never ventured into Marge's garden!

They checked the special boxes every day to see if they had any messages. But there was none except for one from Fifi, asking if they were OK, and one from Forest asking if they had found any more mousee at the farm.

They had just returned from chatting with Culin and were having a little nibble on some tuna and biscuits when the box started buzzing. Saffy's mummy went to answer it. The screen flashed, and Harry's mummy's face appeared! "Hi Hanny, how are you? Everything OK with Harry and Saffy? Have they been good together? I hope they haven't given you any trouble. We arrived home last night, had a great time at the Dirty Dog Show, you know. And then …" Harry's mummy babbled on. Saffy's mummy giggled and said everything had been fine apart from having to clear up the mess in the kitchen after the chickens got in and smashed their eggs all over the floor, and Saffy had spilt nail vanish all over the bathroom. The most exciting thing she said that happened was someone had blown up an old shed at the bottom of the field, and no one knew who or why!

"Really? The shed blew up?" Harry's mummy couldn't believe it. "So I was wondering," she continued, "can I come and collect Harry now? Would that be OK?"

"It's OK, but I can bring him back to you if you'd like? I am sure he would like to go in pawshee again, wouldn't you Harry? I will bring him home this afternoon, and we can have a good natter."

Home! He was going home! Harry wasn't sure how he felt about that. He wanted to see his mummy, but he would miss Saffy so much!

"Harry, I don't want you to go home," said Saffy mournfully. Her golden eyes were wet, and her whiskers drooped.

"I don't want to leave you, Saffy, but Mummy is home, and she might need me. I'm sure I can come back to see you, or you could come to see me." Harry tried to be cheerful.

"I suppose so. Harry. You will need to take your special box with you and your bag. And don't forget your Star of Bravery!"

So whilst Saffy's mummy was getting ready to take Harry home, Harry and Saffy ran off to the human washing room and into the hidey-hole. There they affixed Harry's bag to him and checked to make sure the special box was working. Saffy rubbed Harry close. "We will be together again soon, Harry. Don't worry. And we can Pawtime every day, just like we used to!"

"Harry, are you there? Where are you? We need to go now," called Saffy's mummy. Harry and Saffy head bumped and ran out to see if the Pawschee was already outside.

It was, and Harry remembered how worried he was about going in the Pawschee. Now he had been up a beanstalk, on a caterpillar, and in a jelliwobbler. His world had expanded so much!

"Come on, Harry. In you get! And see you later, Saffy. I won't be long," said Saffy's mummy as she sat in the Pawshee. Its tin lid was down, and they were ready for the road!

Off they roared as Saffy sat at the door, her tail waving, and her eyes twinkling in the sunlight. *Ahhh,* Harry thought, *I hope I am back soon to sleep on the blanket tower with my lovely Saffy.*

The Pawschee enjoyed the open countryside. In no time at all, they were driving into Harry's road and up Harry's drive. His mummy was outside waiting for him. And with a cry of delight, she ran to the Pawschee and scooped Harry out of the car. Saffy's mummy laughed to see such happiness from both of them as Harry purred loudly with delight as his mummy hugged him tight!

"Oh, I have missed you, Harry! Let's go and have some tea, shall we, Hanny?" They walked down the path to Harry's house. He was *home*!

Epilogue

Harry was getting used to the dirty doggos hanging around the house. He had even learnt to hiss back at Lion. Now that he was an agent, he decided he had to be much braver! He and Saffy Pawtimed every day. He still missed her very much, but her mummy said that Saffy could come and stay with him, so he was looking forward to that.

He had already checked his special box that day, and no messages had come in. He had just finished Pawtiming with Saffy. They had played fishy fishy, and as usual, Saffy won. He heard a buzzing. He looked under the cushion, where he hid his special box. and there was a message!

Agent Harry
New Mission Calling.
Prepare for the Fennec Foxes

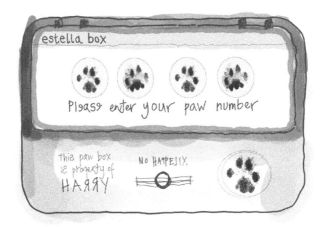

Harry stared at the screen. He couldn't believe it. What did it mean? He would call Saffy and see if she had had the same message.

Pawtime Pawtime, "Saffy, are you there?"

"Yes, Harry. Are you OK?" answered Saffy.

"I have had a message, Saffy. Have you? What does it mean, Saffy?" His tummy was buzzing again.

"I have had the message as well, Harry," replied Saffy. "It's very exciting. It means we are off to Egyptland for mission Fennec Fox!"

Agent Harry and Saffy will return!

Glossary

Apaw: When something doesn't smell right on your whiskers. "Something had gone apaw."

Beefburger: A giant black cow that lives on the farm. They also come in other colours.

Bedroom blanket tower: The best place to sleep. You can climb all the way to the top of all the blankets on top of the hooman clothes storage place and be the king or queen of the hooman house.

Blowing machine: This is what mummies use to dry their head fur.

Bookee: Exactly what you are reading!

Bombee: Our variety is a smoke bombee, a small ball, like an eggie, that explodes to make smoke and confuse the rattus rattus.

Box: The black picture that comes to life when it is fed lickelectricity, and then it shows coloured pictures and words.

Buggels: This is when you have an imposter in your box, a naughty flea who is spying on you.

Caterpillar: The long choo-choo hoomans take to go to work. We think the hoomans call it a train.

Catnav: This is how we smell and feel our way around with our whiskers.

Dinosaurs: The feathery birdbrains that run around the garden, lay the eggies that mousee can be made out of, and that also steal our fud.

Dirty: This is the fluffy white animal thing that lives in Harry's house. Harry's mummy calls this a doggo or a dog. When the dirties do their spinning, they catch all the dirty, muddy things in their furballs.

Doggos: Crazy canines that bark a lot.

Dragonfly Mouse: This is a mousey thingy without a tail or fur. It has four wings and flaps around very fast, like flutter, flutter, flutter.

Dust Monster: These live under Saffy's mummy's bed. All the fur and the fluff and the mummy hair fur collect in a ball under the furniture.

Eggies: The little round jewels the mummies have for breakfast or to make us custard.

Fishanga: This is a special fishtail balancing game, where you stack up the sardines.

Fishy Fishy: A cat game that is played using the box. You chase the fishy around the screen.

Furballed: This is when all the fur gets stuck in your throat, and it makes you cough and splutter a dust monster onto the floor.

Furbrush: This is the brush hoomans use on their head fur.

Fud: Delicious eating stuff that hoomans call food.

Happeelix: This is our favouritest ever fud. We love it on its own or as a topping to our breakfast or dinner.

Holiday Shoppee: This is the shoppee that Harry's mummy goes to buy the exciting holiday fuds that we eat on special days with Daddy Mo.

Honey-Honey Approach: This is the soft, soft, *meoooww, purr* approach that the lady cats use to charm the boy cats and the hoomans.

Hooman: This is an animal, like the mummies, that stands on their back legs and always use the fur brush on his or her head. We don't understand why they don't use their front paws.

Hooman Catflap: This is the big door in the housey that the hoomans go in and out of.

Horsey (verb): To horsey; to run as fast as you can and gallop like a pony.

Identifox: This is the national foxy database of all the known foxes in the United Kingdom and abroad.

Jelliwobbler: A car-like thing that flies in the sky with huge arms, longer than Harry's tail.

Kitty-Litty Tray: This is our special digging place. We don't talk about it; it's very private.

KFC: This is the team of chickens that live in the chicken eggy cage, also known as the small building in the backyard.

Lickelectricity: This is the invisible waves of mousey energy that power the box and Pawtime.

Mousey: A cat game played using the box. It is like Fishy Fishy, but you have to find the hidden mouseys instead.

Mousee: A strong alcoholic drink that makes your paws wobbly.

NCA: National Cats Agency. It is our boss cat's management team.

Pawschee: A very, very fast car with big black eyes and a short tail. Saffy's mummy has one.

Pawcraft: This is our special spy tools and activities that only the spy cats know how to do.

Pawmission: This is our special mission that Professor Maurice Mole and Stella sent us on to defeat the rattus rattus and Vulpes Syndicate.

Pawscibing: This is, very simply, when we write things with our paw pens.

Pawtime (verb)**:** To talk with each other through the box.

Purveillance: This is special undercover work that we do when we are hiding from baddies, following them undercover, with our whisker sensing.

Rattus Rattus: These are the very nasty, sneaky, beady-eyed, fat, and long-tailed mouseys. They smell of rotten fishy and mouldy straw.

Rattigans: This is another name for rattus rattus.

Seafurball Tablet: This is a special medicine tablet that cats can take to stop the furballing on a rocky journey.

Snax: This is what we eat between our breakfast and our dinner to keep the tummy rumbles at bay.

Special Box: This is like the hooman box but a special one for spy cats

Spiders Web: This is powered by the lickelectricity, and is the web of secret tunnels through which special information travels, allowing us to order Happelix on the box.

Vulpes Syndicate: This is the nasty group of foxes who have come together to create a crime gang. They are very dangerous. Do not approach these fox types.

Wiggle Sticks or Wigglers: These are the special lock-breaking and entering sticks that we use to open doors and spy holes.

Wood-burny box: This is the box, without lickelectricity, that our mummies put the wood in to keep the housey nice and warm and toasty.

About our mummies

Hannah Smart

Lynn Morsy

When Boris made a lockdown, our mummies stayed at home,
It was the best year ever, as this boookee now has shown.

We had our mummies all day long, for strokes and Happeelix,
They moved their work online, from 9am to 6.

Harry's mummy **Lynn**, makes transport strategies,
Saffy's mummy, **Hanny**, makes pictures of masterplannies.

They both met Aunty Julie, their business lady coach,
They went on the boxy thing and talked busy-ness approach.

Then the mummies realised, that they were both crazy cats, and so,
they started to write our story in their mini box whhhatttssssats.

The mummies become great friends, talking every day,
to check "how are you **Harry**? **Saffy**, are you both ok????"

They have a love of stories, to take away life stress,
Harry's mummy likes the writing; Saffy's mum - the drawings best!

And so, they came together to tell our story, just for you.
That is how this boookee came - we hope you love it too!

Harry
x

Saffy
x

Lightning Source UK Ltd.
Milton Keynes UK
UKHW040831250522
403501UK00002B/57